DARK EDEN BOOK TWO

SCARS
OF
SEDUCTION
AND
SACRIFICE

J. EMBER HINTZ

SCARS OF SEDUCTION AND SACRIFICE
Copyright 2023 by J. Ember Hintz

Cover Design by MIBLART
Edited by Beth Lawton at VB Edits
Formatting and interior design by Specter Publishing

ISBN: 978-1-958602-00-3 (ebook)
ISBN: 978-1-958602-01-0 (paperback)

To my mom
for introducing me to bodice-ripping romance early on,
which led to my obsession with morally gray anti-heros

PROLOGUE

Liam

THE HORIZON DISAPPEARED THE day my dead girlfriend ripped a hole in the universe and crashed my personal purgatory. She landed like a bomb on the beach, leaving a crater that could have swallowed a damn dump truck. The impact sent up a mushroom cloud of smoke and ash that settled over the ocean, blotting out the line between sea and sky.

My eyes watered as I forced my vision to shift. The enhanced forecaster sight allowed me to see the energy pulsing through everything—earth, water, air. It should have resulted in a psychedelic explosion of color and chaos. The only thing I'd ever been able to see when I scanned this fake fucking paradise was a landscape painted in shades of oil and ash. Even with my enhanced eyesight, I couldn't penetrate the screen of smoke that sat just beyond the reach of my gift.

There was something out there, beyond the boundary of our prison. Something ancient and ravenous biding its time. I could feel it in the back of my brain the same way I could feel the sun on my skin. Hot and prickly. The dark presence had been my only companion in this hell.

Until now.

Chapter One

VAZA

The goddess of death was a greedy bitch. Her rancid scent kissed everything in Eden. It slicked my skin and hair like an oily stain and shoved up my nose despite the moss I'd stuffed in my nostrils. The smell was a small price to pay to remain invisible. No one looked twice at the pungent cloaked figures removing bodies from the streets under the cover of night.

I tugged my hood into place and pressed into the shadows as the collectors passed. Their cart groaned under the weight of its rotting cargo. Thuribles dangling from poles on the back rattled softly, expelling a trail of incense that did little to mask the stench.

I followed its slow descent to the caves beneath the city. Ancient Eden had thrived in the time before the wasting. Before the ice melted and the ocean bloomed with toxic algae that forced our ancestors out of the water. Few survived after being exposed to the red tide. What started as a sore throat and stuffy nose became a wheezing cough and quickly turned into weeping pustules in the gills and lungs until the afflicted drowned in their own mucus.

The body cart lumbered into the mouth of the catacombs, and I darted toward the narrow ledge along the cliff. Waves pounded the wall below, sending tremors through the rock. One slip, and I'd plummet to the angry sea below. I glanced back to ensure no one followed before rounding the corner to the hidden alcove. The tightness in my chest eased once I was out of sight under the overhang where the air smelled of salt and sunbaked stone and was easier to breathe.

I squeezed into the glowing crystal-encrusted fissure at the back of the niche and found the first anchor. The icy blue shards gave off a pale light long into the night after being charged by the grueling sun. They jutted out from the vertical shaft like brittle daggers. I'd learned the hard way which ones were strong enough to support my weight. My feet found the next secure hold, and I descended into the dark heart of the island.

I lowered myself from the ceiling onto the shoulders of a goddess and jumped to the floor with a thud. The jolt activated my bioluminescent markings, and I unlatched the buckles that held my leather armor in place. The soft glow from my chest bathed the figures at the center of the shrine in a soft blue-green light. They were identical aside from their ages, which ranged from maiden to crone.

The Nūkiri had been feared and revered in equal measure when they ruled ancient Eden. Now they were just crumbling relics. Forgotten deities dethroned by the Order of Wu'uru, who'd done everything in their power to erase all but the worst parts of the goddesses' legacy. *Fucking zealots.*

The only thing the Order couldn't erase was the Nūkiri's cursed gift from my soul. Their eyes followed me as I crouched at their feet and pried a loose tile from the floor. I reached in and extracted a wooden box.

As the only fertile females in Eden, queens were afforded every luxury—fine clothes, unlimited rations, private apartments in the House of Blood. We had everything except our freedom. Slaves to our duty from birth to death.

Queens were forbidden from leaving our chambers without our veils and were escorted to and from the temple under armed guard. We rarely interacted with anyone other than each other and the priestesses who served us. They helped us bathe and dress and delivered our food. As our handmaidens, they expressed our scent glands and prepared us for the death and mating rites that consumed our lives.

I plucked a vial from the box and tucked it into my cleavage. Still on my knees, I stashed the remainder of my dwindling supply of frenzy in the ground and replaced the tile at the Nūkiri's feet. Even though it was their magic that cursed me to my fate, I bent forward and touched my forehead to the floor. They'd been keeping my secret safe since the night I'd tried to end my life after my first mating. The night the wraith was born.

My hands found every familiar notch as I climbed out of the hidden shrine. I ducked behind an empty body cart as it exited the catacombs under a cloud of white smoke. The sickly sweet incense tightened my lungs as I helped push it up the steep incline. I slipped down a dark alley when we reached the lower city, where anything could be bought and sold for the right price.

Sweat trickled down my chest beneath my leathers as I adjusted my hood, careful to keep my face hidden. Unlike the frigid caverns, Eden radiated heat even in the dead of night. I couldn't wait to strip off the layers, sink into a cold bath, and scrub the scent of death from my skin. I wore it so often I'd grown nose-blind to the smell.

My scout hadn't let me down yet. I paid her well, but loyalty shifted like sand in the direction of good coin. Io was the best spotter in the lower city and never failed to deliver a mark. I headed for the darkest part of the alley, an area untouched by the hazy glow from the streets on either end, where I could see anyone who approached.

A tall figure stepped out of the shadows; his fluid movements were far too sure to be an addict. I tightened my fist around the hilt of my dagger as he approached with the slow stride of a predator trying not to scare away his prey. His nostrils flared as he scented the air and stopped abruptly ten paces from me, halted no doubt by my stench.

"You're the wraith." A statement, not a question. His deep voice dripped with authority. The kind used to giving orders and being obeyed.

I spat on the cobblestones, buying myself a few extra seconds of threat assessment. There were three kinds of buyers in the slums. The special occasion users were the least problematic and all too grateful to pay whatever I asked for a dose of pure frenzy. The entrepreneurs liked to waste my time haggling for a better price so they could cut and resell the drug outside the bathhouses. Negotiations could be tense, but few would risk pissing off their supplier. The addicts were the most dangerous—so desperate to escape into a frenzy they'd gut you for a taste.

This male was none of the above, and he wasn't from the lower city. His sleeveless tunic and linen trousers were far too clean to belong to someone in lower Eden. His dark hair was pulled back in a tight knot, and his beard was trimmed short in the style favored by males of the noble houses. But his muscular physique and bronzed hide were that of someone familiar with hard labor.

"What's a pretty courtier doing skulking about with the salt eaters?" I asked, forcing my voice lower. The noble houses were the only ones who could afford fresh meat. The rest of the city had to make do with cured scraps.

"Waiting for you." The corner of his mouth twitched as he took a step closer.

Another bead of sweat rolled between my breasts. "Do yourself a favor and fuck off to the upper city before someone relieves you of the coin weighing your belt down."

Another step. "Not until I have what I came for."

I unsheathed my blade beneath my cloak. Something about him was off. "I'm afraid I don't have what you need, friend. If you're desperate for a good time, try Nix's bathhouse down by the docks. She's an ice mage. Her pools are always clean and ready."

Cursed with thick thighs and scarred lungs, I could not claim speed as one of my strengths. The male in front of me was long and lean. If I tried to run, he'd outpace me in a stride.

My eyes flicked to the rooftops. The buildings that circled the lower city resembled the jagged teeth of a gorzin's maw, ready to snap shut at any moment and swallow Eden whole. Half the red clay structures had collapsed from neglect. The other half leaned at precarious angles that made them difficult to scale if you didn't know every hand and foot hold by heart.

"I think you have exactly what I need, *wraith*." He'd erased the distance between us without making a sound. He was so close I could see the fine stitching of his tunic in the dark. The swirling pattern and silver threads marked him as a member of the House of Salt, shield mages with the ability to hold your body under their will while you were in physical proximity. "Your scout said you're the only dealer in the lower city with access to uncut frenzy. That you have a supplier in the House of Blood with direct access to the queens."

"If she told you where to find me, she'll demand a referral fee for sending a rich courtier my way. I'll have to charge you extra to cover the cost." I waited for the warning prickle of his gift against my skin as I extended my claws and reached up to trace the deep, open V of his tunic, unsure if I could react quickly enough to rip out his throat before he clamped his shield around me.

"She's already received generous compensation for her services." His gaze dropped to where my fingers skated over the triangle of exposed skin and soft hair on his chest. I did not know how he could bear standing so close to me when I smelled like a corpse.

"In that case, the cost just doubled since I'll need to find a new scout."

The muscle along his jaw pulsed as he grabbed my wrist and backed me against the wall. "Who's your contact in the House of Blood?"

I positioned the tip of my dagger against his ribs. He released my arm and pressed his palm to the rough wall behind me. I yanked the leather purse from his belt with my free hand. "Information doesn't come free. I only answer questions for coin, and I require payment in advance." Everyone in the slums had a price. I had no intention of revealing any more than he already knew thanks to Io. I just needed to play along until I could get out of range of his gift.

"There's more than triple the asking price in that purse."

I tested the weight before slipping it into the pocket of my cloak. He wasn't lying. "You just bought yourself one vial and two truths."

"Who are you?"

"A survivor destined to do my duty to the dead." Another trickle of sweat ran between my breasts. I gestured to my traditional black cloak and leathers worn by the body collectors. A job only open to those who'd survived the wasting.

The courtier leaned down and brushed his nose over the shell of my ear. His trimmed beard tickled my cheek. "I don't believe you." He made a guttural sound that may have been a growl or a curse, and I refused to acknowledge the way it made my insides go molten. "Body collectors smell like death. You smell like salt and sin, little wraith." His voice came out rough, like it was grinding against the edge of restraint. The bioluminescent stripes on his chest began to glow with desire.

Fuck.

I fished the vial of pheromones from between my breasts. The stopper had come loose and leaked the concentrated aphrodisiac all over my chest. As a queen, I was immune to mating pheromone. A few drops, however, was all it took to send most males into a mindless mating frenzy.

The gold flecks in his green eyes flared as he plucked the half-empty glass tube from my fingers. It happened so fast I told myself I'd imagined it. "Which queen did this come from?"

"How should I know?" I lied. "I'm just a courier."

"Who's your supplier? Is it a priestess or someone in the Queen's Guard?" He still had me pinned against the wall.

I shoved the tip of my blade into his gills. Blood bloomed where it pierced his tunic and flesh. Not deep enough to kill him. Just enough to prevent him from breathing comfortably and giving chase.

"Two truths and one vial. That was the deal. Our business is concluded, and I'll be taking my leave." I shoved away from him and launched my body at the wall on the opposite side of the alley. My fingers found the first hold, and I offered my thanks to the goddesses as I scaled the cracked clay and hauled my ass onto the roof.

I glanced down at the courtier and could swear the corner of his mouth curled into a smile, or maybe a sneer. It was difficult to tell in the dark.

"Our business is just beginning, *wraith*."

The wind caught my hood as I turned and ripped the tie from my hair, freeing the blue-black strands and whipping them around my face like a veil.

⁊

I scrubbed my skin until it was raw. Until every trace of my scent was gone and I could no longer feel the cascade of the courtier's breath against my neck. *Sin and salt.*

"Why would a noble from the House of Salt risk his life by coming to the slums to score product readily available in the upper city?" I asked.

"He's not the first and he won't be the last," Hemeda said. Her eyes narrowed as I stood from the tub and pulled the priestess's red robes over my head. The heavy fabric clung to my damp body. "They say the high priestess is mixing the nobles' rations of frenzy with eel oil. By the time it trickles down to the lower city, it's been diluted so many times the drug isn't worth much coin. It's only a matter of time before every dealer in Eden starts asking where the wraith gets her supply."

"That doesn't make any sense. Zwara would never do anything to undermine her own power. With the mating rites on hold, why would the high priestess tamper with the only other thing keeping the noble houses loyal to her?"

"I can't pretend to understand your sister's motivations. Even as a youngling, she kept her secrets close to the vest." Hemeda's reedy voice went tight. "You need to be careful, Vaza. You can't keep milking yourself dry to keep up with demand. If Zwara—"

"Let me worry about the high priestess. We need to talk about Io. She told the courtier too much." I nodded to the leather coin pouch on the table. "There's more than enough there to cover your expenses through the next tide. Pay Io what she's owed and hire a mind mage to wipe her memories before you cut her loose."

The healer's wrinkled face pinched as she dipped her head. "Consider it done. You are far too generous, my dear."

I glanced at the mangled stump that used to be the right hand of the most gifted blood mage in Eden. "It's the least I can do. We both know the coin I make selling my scent pays for more than just the meat in your salt box." I crossed to the lone window in the crooked shack and studied the obsidian fortress rising from its rocky island pedestal. A single rope bridge connected it to the western edge of the city. "What have the zealots been up to since my last visit?"

"Belief in the prophecy spreads as fast as the wasting. The Order continues to distribute their pamphlets on the pillars of purity."

"Don't eat raw meat until it's been cured. Don't drink, bathe, or fuck in unclean water. Not terrible advice, all things considered."

"They're also spreading a rumor that the high priestess isn't being transparent about the recent wave of deaths."

They weren't wrong about that either. A queen's sole purpose was to ingest and carry the souls of the dead until they could be reborn. I'd been summoned to participate in the death rites so many times I didn't know how many more souls my clutch could hold.

"There are some," she continued, "who say the algae toxins have spread to the fog that plagues the eastern wharf. Zwara stationed a squad of storm mages there to keep it at bay, which only reinforced the fears thrumming through the lower city."

"What about the Order's recruitment efforts?"

"They're gaining traction in the slums where the death toll has been highest. One of their more outspoken leaders, Brex zurNaga, has been proselytizing about the seven signs. He's all but named Tesk as the *ki'sikilta*. The virgin queen who must be sacrificed to resurrect the god of tides, according to the prophecy."

I wiped the courtier's blood from my dagger and sheathed it at my waist. "Brex zurNaga." I repeated the name, committing it to memory. "Where can I find this dead zealot?" I asked, flashing my fangs.

My old nursemaid clicked her tongue in amusement. "Put your teeth away, my queen. A serpent never reveals her fangs until she's within striking distance. No one gets past the Rift's obsidian gate without an invitation."

"Then I'll find a way to be invited."

"You need to be smart about this. Eliminating one zealot won't alter Tesk's fate."

"One isn't nearly enough, but it's a start."

"They'll kill you before you get close, and this will all have been for nothing. Don't let your death be insignificant."

Tesk lifted her head from my lap and hissed as our handmaiden pinched a swollen gland on my sister's spine.

I grabbed Niva's wrist, knocking the half-full extraction vial to the floor. The bioluminescent stripes beneath her ill-fitting robes flashed with fear, making the red fabric glow. "Hurt her again, and I'll bite off your fingers and feed them to my pets."

Her eyes darted to the tank of color shifting targuls behind me. The tentacled predators were intelligent and easy to train, and I loved giving them treats.

Golden hair as fine as silt spilled around the priestess's gaunt face as she lowered her head. "Apologies, *my queen*. Take as many fingers as required." There was an undeniable challenge in her voice. We both knew the high priestess would find a way to punish me for maiming another one of her healers. Blood mages were hard to come by.

I went to the tank and placed my hand in the water. A spotted targul wrapped its tentacles around my fingers and climbed into my palm. Fresh meat was a rare luxury even in the noble houses.

"How long has it been since you've eaten, Niva?"

Her stomach rumbled as she watched the creature twist around my hand. "Three days."

I bit off its head and threw the remainder of its twitching body back into the tank. The water bloomed red as the other targuls fought over the scraps. "Fetch an ice mage to prepare a bath for my sister, and I'll let you fill your belly when you return."

"I'm not to leave without a full vial." The lack of hesitation in her voice told me her fear of disappointing the high priestess outweighed her gnawing pangs of starvation.

"Go." I picked up the glass tube from the floor and gestured to the door. "I'll finish the extraction and deliver it to Zwara myself."

"Of course. Right away, Queen Vaza." Niva slipped into the hall to go search for an ice mage.

Aside from a full release, ice was the only comfort that could lessen the ache of a needing, and Tesk was approaching the peak of her first heat.

"I would have eaten that," Tesk said. "Why did you throw it back in the tank?"

"To prove a point." I sat behind her and massaged the tension from her shoulders. Her hair was the same iridescent blue-black shade as mine. We were identical in every way, from our pale gray hides and wide hips to our vivid blue eyes. Even the spray of bioluminescent freckles across our chests was an exact match. The only difference was the collection of silver scars that covered my body. One for every male who'd claimed me. Hers would fill in soon enough—if the high priestess ever reinstated the mating rite.

Tesk cut me a look. "Was it really necessary to threaten Niva?"

"It wasn't a threat." I ran the heels of my hands along either side of her spine. A shimmer of golden oil beaded up along the bony ridge.

"Are you suggesting you would've ruined her ability to wield her gift over a mere scratch?"

"A mere scratch is all it takes for the red tide's toxins to enter your system." Tesk groaned as I rolled my hands down her spine again, releasing more of the frenzy-inducing pheromone the high priestess used to manipulate the most powerful males in Eden. One taste of the powerful aphrodisiac was enough to make nobles trade fortune and favor for the privilege of mating a queen.

"I don't know who scares me more, you or Zwara. If she doesn't reinstate the mating rites soon, I might die from the needing. My wrist is so sore from pleasuring myself I can barely move it."

"There are worse things than being in heat," I said.

"Like spawning?"

"Giving souls new life is the best part of our sacred duty." I loved watching my belly swell while Niva and the other priestesses pampered me. The two weeks after each mating rite before I released my spawn were the only times in my life when I felt at peace. Hemeda said the feeling was a side effect caused by the change in my pheromones. I wasn't so sure.

"And the worst part?"

Watching the males who impregnated me take *their* hatchlings away. Queens were too rare and our duty too important to be distracted with caring for the broods we produced. But I didn't tell her any of that. She'd learn soon enough.

Tesk sighed in relief as I made another pass over her back and collected the shimmering liquid weeping from her spine.

"How are you so good at that?" she asked.

"Hemeda taught me before she was sent away. Better?"

Tesk nodded as I helped her into her robe. The black silk clung to her sweat-slick skin. She winced as she rolled her wrist.

"Give me your hand."

Tesk stared at me intently as I massaged her palm. "Are you going to make me ask?"

"Ask what?"

"Where you were last night. I finished the smutty book you gave me." My sister lowered her voice. "When I came to return it, you weren't here, but your escort was still standing guard outside your door."

"It's better you don't know."

"Know what? That you sneak around dressed as a priestess and come back just before dawn smelling like frenzy?"

I stopped massaging her hand and lifted my eyes.

"I hid in your apartment and waited for you to return. Take me with you tonight. I *need* to get laid too. If I can find someone to defile me, I won't be the last virgin queen, and the prophecy won't come to pass. Not with me."

"The high priestess will slaughter any male who dares to touch you outside the rite. Would you doom them to certain death over a bit of ancient nonsense written by a brainwashed zealot?"

"Says the killer queen who ripped out her first mate's throat and maimed a priestess during her first mating."

"I've paid dearly for that mistake." I gripped her hand between mine. "Zwara will never stop punishing me for embarrassing her in front of the entire temple."

Tesk's eyes trailed over my scars. "Does it hurt when they claim you?"

The high priestess took great pleasure in saving the worst males for me—the ones who took pleasure in restraining a female against their will. Always a shield mage. She told me it was a necessary precaution if I went into another blood frenzy. That was gorzin shit. Aside from the zealot, I hadn't harmed anyone in the twelve years since my first mating. I knew the males she paired me with paid extra for the privilege of forcing themselves on a queen. Part of me hated her for it. The other part, a very small part, was grateful she didn't subject the other queens to the same torture. Tesk would never know what it was like to be raped as long as I was there to protect her.

"Not when you have an attentive partner," I said. "Most queens take great pleasure in the rites." Letting her believe I was sneaking out to satisfy my needs was less dangerous than telling her the truth.

Tesk's eyes crawled over my shoulder to our ever-present escorts. "At least tell me how you're getting past the guards."

"I won't help you doom yourself to my fate."

"How is it okay for you to do whatever you want, but not me?"

"There's little Zwara can do to punish me more than she already has," I said. "Unlike me, you have everything to lose. Your virginity is her most valuable asset at the moment. One she'll leverage to reestablish her control over the houses when the current wave of red tides retreats. She'll cruciate you if you undermine her by giving up your clutch before she can sell it to the highest bidder."

"Our sister's wrath is better than being sacrificed to resurrect a dead god."

"Forget about the Order and their ancient nonsense. The targul venom they ingest to maintain their celibacy makes their brains as flaccid as their cocks."

"It may be nonsense to you, but the followers of Wu'uru believe every word of his prophecy." Her face paled as she read aloud from an earmarked page. "When the thirteen become twelve, the *ki'sikilta* will be revealed, and with their sacrifice, the god of tides will be resurrected and deliver Eden from the red tide." Tesk's voice cracked. "If we lose another queen, the Order will come for me."

"Zwara will never let them take you. You're too valuable."

"Unless they offer the highest bid. They're as rich as any of the noble houses. She might sell me to them for the right price. It would need to be more than she could possibly make over a lifetime of breeding me."

"That's not going to happen."

"How can you be so sure?"

"Because I'll end anyone who tries to hurt you." I picked up my black veil and wrapped the gossamer fabric around my face and head, securing it with the heavy pearl circlet.

"Where are you going?"

"To see our sister."

Chapter Two

Liam

I shook off the forecaster's sight and pulled a gentle breeze up the beach to the fern grotto that had become our sanctuary. Our home. The air stirred the silvery blond strands of Renae's hair and sent them dancing across her pale shoulders. She'd tied one of my old T-shirts around her chest. The clothes she'd arrived in had been ripped to shreds during her violent entry into the Void. Renae's makeshift top, however, did little to hide the deep purple bruises that still covered her body three weeks later.

I'd spent the better part of the morning lying in the hammock, studying the delicate shape of her nose as she sat on the ground, hunched over the reeds she'd been stripping and weaving into baskets and lengths of rope. I'd never gotten her nose right, no matter how many times I sculpted her. I hadn't created anything new since she'd arrived, even though I'd spent hours in my glass studio every day. When she asked why she wasn't allowed inside, I lied and told her I didn't like working in front of an audience.

The real reason was locked away in the back of the third drawer of my red toolbox. It contained my purgatory survival kit—a rusted Altoids tin that held a plastic bottlecap, a blue lighter, a Q-Tip, a single needle, and a gram of heroin.

No matter how many times I destroyed my stash or the tool cabinet, the island brought it back day after day, month after month, year after year. When I started using, it replenished itself daily. An endless supply. Always a gram. Never more. Never less. Enough to silence the noise. To help me forget. Now that gram was barely enough to be a maintenance dose. A twice daily prescription to keep the nausea and detox shits at bay.

Renae winced as one of the reeds sliced another ribbon-like cut along her forearm, adding to her growing collection of scars.

"You don't have to do that." I stood from the vine hammock and stretched. Renae's forehead wrinkled as the living hammock unraveled and the vines retreated into the trees. "I can manipulate the plants into anything you want—rope, nets, another hammock. Just tell me what you need, and I'll make it for you in a matter of minutes."

"You have your projects." She gestured to the dome of intertwined branches and vines above us. "This one is mine." Renae ran her blistered fingers over the grass rope. *My gifts may be useless here compared to yours, but I can still be useful.*

Her thoughts filtered through my head even though she hadn't said them aloud. They crept in like a fog. Unlike my forecasting and bio-manipulation abilities, the telepathy thing was one of the gifts I hadn't been able to practice or fully master in the Void. I couldn't stop my mind from reaching for hers any more than I could stop myself from reaching for the drug-induced oblivion that had gotten me through most days before she arrived. So I pretended I didn't know she hated it here or that I hated myself for throwing my sobriety out the window and taking the easy way out.

I squatted down and inspected her work, testing its tensile strength. It was a good fucking rope. "Where did you learn how to do this?"

"I begged my father to take me fishing with him once. He agreed, despite my mother's concern for my wellbeing. It was a disaster. I couldn't wield the pole and my crutches at the same time and took a tumble down the riverbank into the rocks, just as my mother had feared." Renae's jaw tightened, accentuating the hollows beneath her high cheekbones where her face had thinned since crashing into the Void to be with me. Her memory played out across both our minds—a sopping wet girl with steel-gray eyes, bloodied knees, and limp legs using the reeds to drag herself out of the mud while her father watched casually from the shore, refusing to help her as she struggled.

"Cheers to asshole fathers." Another thing we had in common.

She shot me a sharp look that told me to get the hell out of her head. I was supposed to be practicing restraint, putting up barriers to protect my mind from contamination, and focusing my telepathic gift on projecting thoughts and images to her instead. Restraint, however, was a practiced skill. One I'd let slip a long time ago. I pulled my gift back to the periphery of her perception and pushed the image of me building glass walls around myself into her mind.

Renae gave a satisfied nod and added another reed to her rope as she continued. "My father wasn't an asshole. He was a good man. He didn't try to protect me from pain or ridicule like my well-meaning mother. He let me figure out how to do things on my own, and more importantly, he let me fail. My father was the only person who understood my need to prove that I wasn't useless. To him, to my mother. To myself. He also knew I couldn't go home empty-handed, so he sat with me in the mud and taught me how to weave reeds into basket traps and flexible rope. Once we had two traps and a strong line, we tied it off to a tree and let the current do the work while my crutches dried in the sun."

Renae's face lit with a smile that jolted my chest like an electrical shock. I'd only ever seen her smile like that once—the first time I'd taken her surfing, when she'd allowed herself to feel, to be free. Unrestrained and full of emotion, as if an invisible weight had been temporarily lifted. That smile had haunted my dreams during the decade I'd been trapped here alone.

My entire body stilled as my brain raced to memorize the gentle curve of her full lips, the way the skin around her eyes crinkled slightly, and the way her face seemed to come alive for the first time since she'd arrived. Heat throbbed in my palms with the urge to sculpt her like this while the memory was fresh in my mind.

"My father showed me how to lean my chest against the back of the tree and use it as an anchor to hold me up so I could pull in my line without falling on my face and getting dragged downstream. We had trout for dinner that night and the next." Renae's hands stopped working as her lashes fluttered shut. I didn't have to read her mind to know her thoughts had shifted to food.

I didn't have the heart to tell her there were no trout, or crabs, or any other living, breathing things on this island besides us. Like that strong-willed little girl from her memory, it was a lesson she'd need to learn for herself.

"Will you teach me how to weave them?" I asked selfishly. Not because I wanted to make traps or fishing line. I didn't want to break the spell and chase away the brief moment of happiness beneath the mask she wore like a shield.

Renae's fingers grazed mine as she handed me a tough green reed the length of my leg. "You need to remove the rigid spine to make it pliable."

"Isn't that the part that gives the reed its strength?"

"Only when it stands alone. You need a soft, flexible rope that we can tie off. Not one that resists being manipulated." She stripped the leafy parts from another reed and set them aside. "Nothing is wasted, though. We'll use the spines as the ribs of the baskets like so." She laid the stiff spine on the ground in front of her with three others, one on top of another at different angles, and secured them at the center axis with a series of leafy knots to form what looked like the spokes of a wheel. She lifted it from the center, bent it into a bell shape, and proceeded to weave more reeds around the spines in an over-under pattern until she had the beginning of an inverted basket.

I studied the way her blistered fingers bent the tough reeds, the way she clenched her jaw in pain and worked her bottom lip between her teeth in concentration. She was as beautiful as she was stubborn. I had to remind myself that she was *real* and not a phantom sent to taunt me by whatever entity lived beneath the surface of our contrived paradise.

If this Renae was an illusion, she was a damn good one. Real or not, I had no intention of losing her again. I hadn't slept well in weeks for fear she might vanish or get sucked back into the oily black abyss that existed beyond our little bubble of reality the moment I closed my eyes.

"Stop doing that," she said.

"Doing what?"

"Staring at me like I might disappear. It weirds me out when you watch me like that."

"I can't help it. Everything you do fascinates me." I reached out and stilled her hand, turning her palm over and running my fingers over the fresh cuts. "Let me fix these for you. There's no need to torture yourself."

It's the least I deserve. Her unspoken words floated through my head. She was thinking about her sister again. She dreamed about Lucy every night. The recurring nightmare was the only way I knew she was the real Renae. My Renae. The same agony sat in my gut like a lead brick every time I stepped inside her head and watched her nightmare play out over and over. Lucy, Cyrena, and Ziggy—my mother—sacrificing themselves to send her into the Void.

Renae pulled her hand away and fisted her palm. "I don't mind the pain. The blisters will callus eventually. Once they toughen up, I won't feel a thing." Renae plastered a pleasant mask on her face and set her work aside. I wasn't the only one pretending. We both knew some wounds bled forever.

She stood and brushed the bits of leaf and reed from the black boxers that clung to her hips and thighs. "Why don't we take a break? I'm starving."

Electricity crawled over my skin, roping its way around my arms from wrist to shoulder as I followed her inside the bungalow. Just being confined within the walls was enough to trigger my gift. Whatever fight-or-flight instincts I possessed in my slurry of DNA recognized the risk of being stuck inside a house that wasn't a house. A predatory power hummed through everything—the walls, the foundation, the ground beneath us. Renae hadn't noticed it, and I hadn't found the right moment to tell her about the island's invisible inhabitant. No, that was a lie. I hadn't told her because I was selfish. I wanted to tease out whatever brief happiness I could for her while I had the chance. Once she learned the truth, it wouldn't be just her and me anymore. It would be us and the entity that feeds on trauma and despair.

Out of habit, I reached for the endless supply of beer in the fridge, but I stopped myself before my fingers connected with the glass bottle and grabbed two of the blue plastic containers instead.

"The last thing I expected to find in the Void was a tropical paradise with a magic refrigerator that contained an endless supply of regenerating food." Renae peeled the lid off her lunch and poked at it with her fork before taking a bite and swallowing hard. For her, a woman who craved the sensual pleasure of food, eating the same thing every day for an eternity had to be its own kind of hell.

I'd been choking down the salmon, peas, and rice three times a day, every day for more than a decade. Renae had only been here a few short weeks. The shitty menu was the least of the horrors this place could dish out.

She took another bite and pushed the container to the side.

"You'll get used to it." I kissed her temple and pushed the container back toward her. "Eat. You need to rebuild your strength." Her body's self-healing hadn't followed her into the Void. Her full hips and waist had thinned. Her auburn curls had gone stark white from the god-awful way she'd had to separate her soul from her body to get here, even her whiskey eyes had faded to a pale gold. She was the most surreal and beautiful thing I'd ever seen.

"I know. I just miss tacos, and pizza, and doughnuts."

"Now *that* I can help with." I yanked my gift to the surface and projected the flavor of pizza into her mind—the texture of chewy crust, hot cheese dripping with grease from a double layer of pepperoni and the smoky scent of garlic and tomato.

"Did I mention how much I love you?" Renae said, groaning softly as she shoveled a fork full of rice into her mouth.

"Feel free to remind me later, when we're both naked."

Renae bit back a smile as she savored her lunch and traced her fingertips over the horizontal hash marks that covered the top of the table. One for every day I'd spent on the island without her. She stopped and stared at the deep grooves, as if seeing them for the first time. "The marks on the walls are vertical. Why are so many of the marks on the table horizontal?" she asked.

My spine stiffened. "I started counting time with the table. The horizontal lines are the days I looked for a way out of this place." One horizontal hash mark for every time I'd flatlined attempting to escape, only to wake up in my bed the next day, good as new, like in some shitty movie. But I didn't tell her that part.

Her head whipped to mine. "Why did you give up?"

I sniffed and swiped at my runny nose, considering how to explain it without scaring her. It took me four and a half years to figure out the sentient energy controlling this place didn't want me to leave. It provided just enough to keep me alive so it could torture me and feed on my misery. Each time the island claimed my life, it brought me back the next day the same way it brought back the food in the fridge and the cursed red toolbox that offered a different kind of escape. One I eventually accepted. I could blame it on desperation or a moment of weakness, but that was a cop-out. The real reason was simple. Opportunity. There had been no decision or debate involved the first time I gave in and shot up.

"I didn't give up. I accepted defeat. There's a difference."

Renae's shoulders slumped as her fingers floated over the table's gouged surface. "Agree to disagree, she said." *If there's a way in, then there has to be a way out.* Her spine straightened as the unspoken thought flashed to memories of her father so fast I almost missed it.

I grasped the seat of her chair and jerked it to face me, caging her between my arms.

"If there was a way out, I would have found it. Don't you think I tried? I would have done anything to get back to you."

I'd died hundreds of times on this cursed pile of sand, and I wasn't about to risk Renae's life to prove something I already knew. Not when there was a better than good chance that the island wouldn't bring her back the next time it reset. "It's better if you stay inside when I'm in the studio," I said.

Fire sparked in her golden eyes. "Is that an order?"

I released the death grip I had on her chair and forced my shoulders to relax. She'd bound her soul to mine to bring me back from the brink of death. The sacrifice she made to save my life had also bound her to my will. I'd only compelled her once—when I'd forced her to leave me to keep her safe. But I couldn't stay away. She was my anchor. I had begged for her forgiveness and promised I would never compel her again. As much as I wanted to confine her. I refused to order her to stay. Besides, there were other ways to keep her inside.

The air went staticky as I pulled in a charge. "I'm just trying to keep you safe."

Renae gathered our dishes and stood. "I'm perfectly capable of taking care of myself."

Thunder rumbled outside as I gestured to the bruises she refused to let me heal. "You don't have a genetically enhanced superhuman husk anymore, and you're not some broken child who needs to belly-crawl through the mud to prove she's stronger than she looks."

Renae flinched at the verbal jab, and I regretted the words the moment they fell out of my mouth.

She gave me her rigid back as she washed the plastic containers.

I stepped behind her and reached out to smooth my hand over her bare arm, but she spoke before I could apologize for being an ass.

"Go. I think we could both use some space."

I fisted my left palm to hide the heroin withdrawal tremor. "Promise me you'll stay in the house. There's a storm coming, and I don't want you to get caught out there alone."

"I'm not afraid of a little rain."

"I'm serious, Renae. Today isn't a good day to go for a run."

She spun to face me, her hands dripping water on the floor. "You're right. I'm not a child and I'm not a pet either. This rule that I need to stay in the house when you're gone is ridiculous. You can't just tie me up like a dog to keep me from wandering off."

"Don't tempt me, chica." My brain conjured up all the ways we could put her little rope to good use, and none of them had anything to do with keeping her inside. I folded her into my arms and pressed a kiss to the top of her head, breathing in the salt and coconut scent of her hair. "Keep working on your baskets. As soon as I finish in the studio, we can go for a run on the beach together." The island had tortured me on a daily basis before she arrived. I had no intention of letting her wander around out there alone.

Chapter Three

My escort followed three paces behind as I descended the spiral staircase at the center of the House of Blood. The red stone castle stretched to the sky and sat like a crown on Eden's highest peak with all the other noble houses, looking down on everything else. The temple sat on the opposite side of the upper city, with its obnoxious façade—a giant monument to the god of tides. No matter where you were, from the balconies of the queen's keep to the coral rag shacks in the lower city and all the way down to the Rift, you could see the golden-eyed effigy standing watch over Eden.

The only time a queen was seen in public was during the procession to the mating rite. Even then, our faces were completely covered. When our presence was required for anything else, we were escorted through the ancient tunnels under the city.

My skin pebbled at the cool kiss of air against my bare shoulders as we entered the subterranean passageway. It was a welcome relief from the heat of my chambers. I'd dressed in a backless shift. The flowing fabric hung from thin straps at my shoulders and grazed the floor. Designed for idle lives and easy access to our spines—not an angry march through a freezing tunnel.

I hadn't planned on leaving my rooms until I'd figured out how to get an impossible invitation to the Rift. It wasn't like the Order hosted public functions or gave tours of the impenetrable obsidian fortress that occupied its own island. The Order Guard was legendary for its ruthlessness. Anyone who attempted to cross the bridge without an invitation was met with a swift death or locked in the prison deep beneath the Rift, never to be seen again.

Hemeda was right. No matter how determined I was to gut Brex zurNaga for attaching my sister's name to the prophecy, not even the wraith could sneak into their stronghold. I was immune to the red tide, but the wasting had ruined my gills and ability to breathe underwater. Scaling the sea cliffs wasn't an option unless I hired a storm mage and a boat to navigate the rough sea. Too risky. Io's loose lips were a reminder that I couldn't trust another outsider. Times were too desperate to expect loyalty from anyone.

My only way into the Rift was to manipulate the high priestess into helping me. Zwara didn't do anything that wasn't in her own best interest, and I knew better than most that her favor and her wrath came at a steep price.

A pair of temple guards dipped their heads as we approached the wall of ice that plugged the tunnel exit beneath the temple. The ice cracked as a mage in pale blue robes placed her hand on the frosted surface. As it melted, the water remained suspended and crawled away from the opening in snakelike tendrils. I'd passed through the ice door every day of my life. Not so much as a drop of water had ever fallen on me. I still held my breath every time.

I exhaled as I crossed the threshold on the other side and followed my escort up the spiral staircase inside the monument to the god of tides, which served as the high priestess's rectory. There were no floors or landings, only a dizzying set of marble steps leading to Zwara's chambers inside his empty head.

A pair of carnelian doors greeted us at the top. The hair on the back of my neck prickled with awareness in a way that told me I was being watched. I glanced behind me and found Zwara's personal consort.

The air mage possessed three individual bodies—two males and one female—all linked by one mind. All stunningly beautiful and with ebony eyes and dark-gray hides that allowed them to blend into the shadows. Their gift allowed them to manipulate air currents to propel sailing ships or even fly. They could also rip the breath from your lungs.

As a paid companion with access to the private chambers and proclivities of high-ranking clients in each of the noble houses, Kor was also Zwara's favorite spy.

"Queen Vaza requests an audience with the high priestess," my escort announced.

The air shifted as three bodies peeled away from the dark corner where they'd been hiding.

"Zwara's preparing for a procedure and has asked not to be disturbed," Kor's female form said. A gentle breeze caressed my spine in a forbidden touch as their male counterparts circled around me. "We'd be happy to entertain you while you wait."

"I believe she'll make an exception." I held up the vial of frenzy I'd collected from Tesk.

"Your sister is in no mood to be challenged today," Kor said in a warning tone, as if it was somehow different from any other day.

I bit back my reply and opened the door. No luxury had been spared in Zwara's chambers inside the statue's hollow skull. From the footed glass tub to the canopied bed big enough to accommodate her and all three of Kor's forms, the furnishings were extravagant.

A tank of scuttle crabs sat on the opposite side of the room between two jeweled-glass windows made to look like the god of tides' glowing yellow eyes keeping watch over the temple's mating pools and the city below.

Zwara sat in the center of the floor with her hands on her knees, palms facing up, and heavy robes puddled around her like a pool of blood. Her blackened fingers—stained by the liquid silver she used to help amplify her gift—twitched at the interruption. Zwara's gift didn't come as easily to her as it did to others. She'd always had to meditate to channel her magic before a major operation.

Her neck made a soft popping noise as she stretched her head to the side, sending a cascade of short blue-black hair over her face. Unlike Tesk and me, who kept ours long and pinned securely beneath our veils, Zwara had always worn hers cropped at the chin. She wasn't identical to Tesk and me, but there was no denying the resemblance in her pale-gray hide and icy blue eyes.

We were the only three souls in our brood to survive being spawned in contaminated water. I was the first to hatch and the only one inflicted with the wasting. My sisters' eggs had been frozen to rid them of the deadly toxins. The extended incubation in ice delayed the onset of Tesk's first heat. It also blunted Zwara's gift, but she didn't let it stop her from clawing her way to the top of the House of Blood.

Zwara didn't bother opening her eyes when she spoke. "The next time you try to bribe one of my priestesses, I'll withhold *your* rations for three days."

"Her hands were trembling from starvation. She cut Tesk three times."

"Niva was being tested." Zwara pinned me with a sharp look as she pulled on her robes. "You can leave the frenzy on my medicine chest on your way out."

I set the glass vial on a tray next to an exquisite set of glass scalpels. I lifted one and ran the pad of my thumb along its sharp edge. A thin line of blood welled on my skin. Glass was an impractical material for a blade. It dulled too quickly and was easily broken. But it was nonconductive and the only material that didn't interfere with a priestess's gift. I leaned against the crystal cabinet of oils and tinctures Zwara used to enhance her magic.

"Why were you testing the mage? Did she do something to disappoint you?"

"You need not concern yourself with such things. Niva won't scratch our sister again. Rest assured that the safety and comfort of the queens have always been my priority."

The silver scars covering my body were a testament to her blatant lie. It took every bit of the practiced composure Hemeda had drilled into me as a youngling to keep my anger in check.

"Tesk won't be comfortable or *safe* until you reinstate the rite. All this talk of the prophecy has her on edge. The sooner you reopen the temple pools, the better."

Zwara's face pinched as she rose to her feet. "If I reinstate the mating rite, how do you suggest we feed the hatchlings? They'll need meat."

"There's plenty of meat rotting in the catacombs. Salt curing removes the red tide toxins from fish."

"Are you suggesting I feed salted corpses to hatchlings and teach them to crave Kateri flesh?"

"It wouldn't be the first time we reverted to cannibalism to survive. It was standard practice when the Nūkiri ruled Eden. Why should the bodies of the dead go to waste when they could help sustain the living?"

"The goddesses' disrespect for the dead got them executed. To even suggest bringing back such a thing would cause public outrage. The Order would have every right to call for a vote of no confidence by the noble houses and have me removed. You have no idea how difficult it is to keep this city from ripping itself apart during an epidemic. Maintaining public support is crucial."

"If you won't reinstate the mating rites, send me to the Rift to study the prophecy. The Order has the largest library in Eden. If I go as your emissary, they can't deny me access to their religious repository."

"Since when are *you* interested in the prophecy?" Zwara laughed as she cleared a pile of old scrolls from the stone examination slab she used as a desk. She rarely worked on patients herself, reserving her gift for high-ranking members of the noble houses who could afford discreet treatment.

"I'm interested in anything that affects Tesk. I'd be as safe there among the celibate zealots as I am in the House of Blood. They're still a part of the church."

"In doctrine only. The Order put the House of Blood in charge of the queens for a reason when they overthrew the Nūkiri. They don't want anything to do with the rites or the work it takes to manage the hatchlings. Their extreme devotion to the prophecy makes them a tenuous ally at best."

"All the more reason to let me be your eyes and ears inside the Rift."

"You're a queen, Vaza. Not a spy."

"Exactly. They would never suspect—"

The red doors to Zwara's chamber swung open.

"Excuse the interruption, darling," Kor's female form said with a smirk. "Your patient is waiting in the narthex and causing a bit of a scene."

"Send them up. Vaza and I are finished here."

I dipped my head at the dismissal and moved toward the door. In my desperation, I'd made a mistake. Zwara didn't grant favors. She sold them the same way she sold mating contracts for the rite. I'd have to find another way into the Rift.

"Stay," Zwara said. "You've always been an avid student of history. It's time you had a lesson in politics. Stand there." She pointed to one of the god of tides' golden eyes. A reminder that queens were to be seen and not heard. I assumed the position, clasping my palms in front of me and lowering my gaze to the floor in practiced obedience.

Zwara let out a heavy breath as the sound of boots echoed up the stairwell. Whoever her patient was, they'd come with an escort and had the kind of coin that could buy the high priestess' personal attention.

"Prince Hazi, it's an honor to be of service. I'm so sorry you had to wait." Zwara's voice dripped with feigned civility.

I kept my chin down and lifted my eyes to peer through the dark folds of my veil. I'd never seen the infamous prince who'd given up his claim to the House of Salt's throne. His silver-blond hair was pulled back in a tight knot, revealing the shaved sides of his scalp. Ancient geometric script covered his pale hide from head to foot. He and another massive male in matching sleeveless gray training leathers supported an injured female between them. She held a wad of fabric to her ribs. A crimson stain bled through the cloth, wetting her fingers and the end of her golden braid. Her pinkish-gray hide carried a deathly pallor.

"Thank you for seeing us on short notice, your highness." His brow wrinkled as he glanced down at the injured female.

"How did this happen?" Zwara asked, taking a step toward her.

"It's my fault, your highness," the other male said. "I'm afraid I was a bit overzealous during our sparring session."

My head snapped up at the sound of his deep voice, and my eyes landed on the broad-shouldered courtier I'd stabbed the night before. *You smell like salt and sin.* A bead of frenzy slid down my spine. How many times had I imagined his words as I'd coaxed out my own pleasure before falling asleep?

His nostrils flared as his muddy green gaze swept over me. Half of his dark shoulder-length hair was tied back with a leather cord. My heart raced at the recognition that flashed across his rugged features. I told myself it was only my pheromone he recognized, not the wraith.

"My queen." I didn't miss the wince he tried to hide as he gave me a stiff compulsory bow before dragging his eyes away and returning his attention to my sister. "I'm afraid the wound is grievous. The queen should be sent away and spared the gory details."

"Queen Vaza is no stranger to the sight of blood. She stays."

"We paid handsomely for privacy, your highness," the prince said.

"You're welcome to wait in line with the sick to see a blood mage in the temple if you don't like my terms."

Prince Hazi shot the dark-haired courtier a questioning look. Something was off about the entire situation. Why would a prince defer judgment to a subordinate? Why would the courtier hide his own injury from the high priestess?

The courtier squared his shoulders. "That won't be necessary."

"I'm so glad we're all in agreement." Zwara gestured to the stone slab and asked the courtier's injured companion to take a seat.

A buzzing sensation kissed my skin as the courtier dropped a shield of silence over my perception. He gave me an apologetic nod, and I had the urge to stab him all over again. The trio clearly didn't want me to hear what the prince was saying to my sister.

I wasn't great at reading lips, but there was no mistaking the nearly empty vial he handed Zwara. My heart raced as she popped the cork and sniffed the contents. The high priestess knew the nuances of every queen's scent, and I had no doubt she recognized it immediately. Her expression, however, gave nothing away. When she spoke, it was to the courtier. Whatever she said made him release his shield from my perception.

"I apologize for the ruse, high priestess. I was working undercover when I was attacked. As Hazi said, I believe you have a traitor in the House of Blood, and I couldn't risk blowing my cover by seeking a blood mage from the temple."

He nodded to his injured companion, and she straightened. Her bandage and wound vanished like they'd never existed. The female winked at me, and I felt a gentle brush at the back of my skull. An apology for the illusion she'd forced into my head. I watched as their leathers shifted from salt gray to ebony, marking them as officers in the Order Guard.

"Ifthere's a traitor," Zwara said, "I'll find them myself. Now kindly ask your companions to leave. I don't work in front of an audience."

My palms went sweaty as I glared at Zwara from beneath my veil. How could she stand there and be civil when the Order had just deceived their way into the temple and her personal chambers?

"We'll be right outside, brother," Prince Hazi said as he shrank toward the door, dragging the uninjured female with him.

"You'll need to disrobe if you want me to assess your injury," Zwara said.

He winced as he reached for the buckles behind him that held his overlapping chest and back plates in place.

"Vaza, help Commander zurNaga remove his armor."

I stilled at the name—zurNaga. *Brex zurNaga.* The delusional zealot who thought that sacrificing my sister to his dead god would end the red tides once and for all.

"Why aren't you moving?" Zwara glanced from me to the commander. "Do you still have her under a shield?"

"I would *never* restrain a female unless it was for her own safety."

My eyes landed on my sister's glass scalpels. They would be cleaner and faster than my claws. I'd have to slit his throat from behind. If he saw it coming, he'd immobilize me before I got the chance to end him. Rivals for the public's devotion, there was no love lost between the church and the Order. Zwara might even help me cover up the murder and say he perished from his punctured lung.

I knew what they called me—heard the whispered question roll through the crowd every time I made the procession to the rite. *Will the Killer Queen strike again?*

Zwara was more likely to say I'd had another episode and let the Order throw me in the prison beneath the Rift to save her own skin. No. I couldn't risk leaving Tesk alone. I glanced back at the scalpels. They were so close.

"*Vaza.*" My head snapped back to my sister, who gave me a warning look. "The commander is waiting."

I unclenched my fists and retracted my claws, ignoring the burn where they'd pierced my palms. It took every bit of focus I had to maintain a relaxed posture as I crossed the room.

The zealot dipped his head in reverence, and I ignored the way my name dripped from his tongue like honey. "You honor me with your assistance, Queen Vaza."

He held his breastplate in place as I circled to his back and made quick work of the buckles with shaking hands.

"You've done this before." A statement, not a question.

My eyes flicked to Zwara, who'd busied herself preparing an ointment. Queens didn't wear armor, and they certainly never had the occasion to undress anyone who did. If she heard the comment, she didn't acknowledge it.

Had he gotten taller? Even if I stood on the tips of my toes, I wouldn't be able to lift the heavy leathers over his head.

He perched his tight ass on the edge of the exam table. More of a lean than a full seat, as if he was hesitant to put himself in a position he couldn't easily defend. The heat from his body radiated like a stone left in the sun as I stepped between his knees and lifted the scaled armor over his head and placed it on the floor.

I sucked in a breath at the sight of his naked torso. A spot of blood darkened a bandage plastered to his gills. A minor wound compared to the arc of scar tissue that cut through his taught muscle from shoulder to gut.

"You survived a gorzin attack," I whispered, unable to stop the words before they left my lips. Enemy or not, I was impressed. Gorzin were triple the size of a Kateri and ten times as deadly. I lifted my hand to touch the puckered flesh as another drop of frenzy slid down my spine. A prickle of power ran up my arm, and my fingers stilled as he wrapped his gift around my hand, holding it in place before I could make contact.

"You know your predators well, my queen." I felt his gaze on my face through the veil and realized I was still standing between his spread thighs, close enough for his breath to rustle the sheer fabric.

"Vaza was obsessed with dangerous creatures when we were younglings." Zwara threw the comment over her shoulder as she ground several ingredients into a paste. "She spent all her free time in the House of Blood's library filling her head with nightmares. Gorzin. Giant targuls. The Nūkiri."

"Some would say a queen is a dangerous creature." The zealot dropped his eyes to my hand, still frozen mid-reach between us, and released his hold. I stepped away from him as Zwara turned and placed two bowls on the stone slab.

"I assure you, Commander, my queens are quite docile. Please don't judge them based on one unfortunate incident. The wasting stole Vaza's ability to breathe underwater. Her mate was warned, and he still attempted to pull her under. She had a panic attack and went into a blood frenzy. Her actions were not her own."

His brow furrowed as he took in the silver bite marks covering my chest and arms. A pair for every set of fangs that had claimed me during the rites. "Apologies, my queen." He brought his fist to his chest and dipped his head. "That wasn't what I was implying. I was referring to a queen's scent. Vials of uncut pheromone are making their way to the lower city."

"I don't understand how that could be dangerous." I spoke softly, in the high tongue of the noble houses, praying he didn't recognize my voice. "It doesn't harm the nobles who take it during the rite."

"Conditions in the lower city aren't as pristine as they are in the temple baths. The effects of the undiluted aphrodisiac have led to an increase in high-risk mating behavior in contaminated pools. The red tide infects twice as many there." His eyes lingered on Zwara's blue-black hair as she packed his wound with the thick poultice she'd made. Every muscle in his torso went taut, accentuating the dark line of hair that ran up the center of his stomach.

"How did you come into possession of the empty vial you brought me?" Zwara asked as she straightened.

"I recovered it from a user at one of the public bathhouses."

Liar. My eyes flicked to his, and I didn't care that he'd caught me ogling him. The vial was half full when I sold it to him. What had he done with the rest? Had he taken it himself? Used it to get off? *Salt and sin.* I bit back the accusation on the tip of my tongue as my spine wept, betraying my arousal at the thought of him masturbating to my scent. Revealing myself as the wraith, however, would do me no favors.

"And what was an officer of the Order Guard doing in a public bath?" Zwara dipped her stained fingers in one of the bowls, coating them to the knuckle in a thick layer of black oil, before investigating his injury.

"There's a shortage of ice mages in the lower city. We send as many as we can spare to help sanitize the pools. I was escorting one when I came across the vial."

"Were you stabbed in the public bath as well?" I asked, daring him to lie again.

His gaze slid to me. "I never said I was stabbed."

"It's obviously a puncture wound," Zwara said. "But it doesn't appear to have damaged anything vital. Had it gone any deeper, it could have been fatal."

"I'll be sure to thank my assailant for sparing my life when I track her down." His brow knit together in a scowl as he glared down at the top of her head.

"You're a shield mage. Why did you let her go?" I asked, more than a little curious about why he hadn't attempted to restrain me with his gift.

"As I said, my queen. I'm not in the habit of holding females against their will." He didn't take his eyes off my sister as she worked on mending his torn flesh.

"How fortunate for your attacker that you were able to show such restraint," I said as I moved casually toward Zwara's medicine chest. "You seem confident that you'll find her again."

"She was covered in frenzy. I was able to track the scent to a shack along the southern cliffs."

My body went still. *Hemeda.* No amount of coin could make her betray me. Of that, I was certain. The old mage would sooner die than give me up. If he'd tortured her...

"It was abandoned when I arrived," he added. "Whoever lived there left in a hurry. The neighbors said it belonged to a body collector. When I plied them with more coin, one admitted to seeing a priestess in red robes visit once a tide, always under the cover of night."

I picked up the empty vial and sniffed the cork, exhaling slowly to release the breath I'd been holding. But the sickly sweet scent that laced the inside of my nose wasn't mine. It was Tesk's. The zealot was right. There was another traitor in the House of Blood. Was that why Zwara was "testing" her priestesses?

"The destitute will say and do anything for coin," Zwara said as his wound closed beneath her blackened fingertips.

"I'd like to interview every priestess with access to the queens, just to be sure."

I smiled behind my veil. The Order had always been vocal in their opposition to Zwara's rule as high priestess. She would never allow them to set foot inside the House of Blood.

"That's not necessary," Zwara said. "I personally vet each of my blood mages before I allow them access to the queens. Their loyalty is above reproach."

"With all due respect, we wouldn't be having this conversation if that were true. I'm afraid I must insist. You're welcome to assign a priestess to sit in on the interviews."

"Unfortunately, every spare mage I have is focused on caring for the sick." Zwara gave me a sidelong glance. "I can, however, spare a queen. Before you arrived, Vaza was telling me how bored she's become with her idle life."

The glass vial slipped from my hand and bounced on the tile floor before shattering at the zealot's feet, splattering them with frenzy.

"I'm so sorry, Commander." Zwara cut me a scathing glance. "Vaza has terrible hand-eye coordination."

"I'm sure the veil doesn't help," he muttered under his breath.

"Come to the House of Blood tomorrow, Commander zurNaga. Once she's done her duty to the dead, Queen Vaza will be happy to entertain you during your visit and sit in on interviews."

Chapter Four

VAZA

THIN SHEETS OF STONE draped from the cave ceiling like folds of golden fabric. I floated on my back and tried to focus on the death rite, breathing in the sulfur-infused steam that carried the souls of the dead into my clutch. Queens were trained to recognize the subtle frequency of each gift and transfer them into a cache of fertilized eggs before spawning an entire pod of storm mages or shields—whatever the high priestess ordered us to bring back.

I hated the males she forced on me during the rite, but I'd never resented doing my sacred duty to the dead—giving a soul's magic new life.

Without a host or physical form to occupy, their energy would eventually dissipate and return to the celestial bodies from which it came. Likewise, a hatchling without a soul would be nothing more than a mindless creature. Queens could incubate and recycle a soul's innate magic, but we couldn't reincarnate memories or who they'd been in a past life.

When the Nūkiri ruled Eden, they'd carried the duty of restoring the dead, but they didn't need the death rite to take in a soul. They could reap it from a living host just as I'd accidentally done during my first rite. Just as they'd done to the god of tides.

The Order believed his soul was still out there, waiting to be restored by the *ki'sikilta*. With his return, we would once again be protected from the red tides that had plagued Eden.

The cloudy-blue pool inside the underground temple was the most beautiful place in Eden. No veils, no whispered slurs. Unlike the pretentious monument above honoring the god of tides, the underground hot spring was as nature intended. Rough and beautiful all at once. The priestesses were fond of bathing in the hot spring when it wasn't being used for the rite.

I swallowed down the metallic essence of a blood mage. A storm mage followed and burned like a shot of fermented kelp as it slid down my throat. Every mage gift had a distinct flavor. My least favorite was the explosion of salt that desiccated my tongue every time I took in a shield. Give me the smoky essence of a mind mage or even the bitter ash of a queen over a throat-clenching shield.

The stronger the gift, the more potent the flavor. My first mate had been a gentle spirit mage. I would never forget the hint of crushed herbs as I sucked out his soul. The story Zwara told the zealot was only partially true. I'd had a panic attack, but I hadn't ripped out his throat in a mindless blood frenzy. I wished it was that simple. Only Hemeda knew the truth—that I'd accidentally killed him with the kiss. She was the one who told me to fake the blood frenzy to cover up what I'd done.

The Nūkiri were reviled for their ability to reap a soul from a living body and claim its power for themselves. The goddesses used their gift to rule with absolute authority, eliminating those who challenged them and demanding frequent sacrifices from the dead. Waking a dormant soul from their clutch granted them temporary magic until the sacrificed spirit was used up. Consumed completely.

The practice ended when the god of tides' disciples, led by the prophet Wu'uru, staged a coup and dragged the goddesses into the bowels of the ancient city. The Nūkiri had never been seen again.

If the Order found out the gift had resurfaced after two millennia, they'd lock me in their dungeon or drop me in a gorzin pit. It didn't matter that I had no idea how I'd sucked out the spirit mage's soul.

I bit back a smile at the thought of how the zealot would taste if I could take his soul. Zwara meant to punish me for bribing her disciple by forcing me to entertain Brex zurNaga. Instead, she'd given me a gift. I no longer needed to sneak into the Rift to take out my enemy. He was coming to me.

"Vaza." The high priestess snapped my name like a whip. "Don't you have somewhere else to be?"

My eyes fluttered open, and I realized the rite was long over. Zwara glared down at me from the edge of the pool.

"Apologies, *your highness*." I dropped my feet to the bottom, stirring up a cloud of white silt as I forced an exaggerated bow. If Zwara thought for a moment that I might enjoy the task she'd given me, she'd yank it away and find someone else to do the job.

"I grant you a favor and you repay me with a shitty attitude?"

"Am I supposed to be excited about spending the day with a brainwashed zealot who thinks our sister should be sacrificed to a dead god?" I climbed out of the pool and let the acolyte wrap me in a black robe.

"Leave us." The acolyte scurried away at her command. Zwara continued once the young blood mage was out of earshot. "You're the one who begged me to make you a spy."

"You and I both know these interviews are a waste of time. Your disciples are loyal to the death. Why would you risk inviting a member of the Order into the House of Blood? What if there is no traitor? He's obviously lying to gain access to Tesk."

The corner of Zwara's mouth curled. "The Order has doubled their recruiting efforts for storm and shield mages in the lower city. I want to know what they're up to. You have my consent to do whatever it takes to seduce information from our new friend."

I flinched, wondering if I'd heard her correctly. "As in—"

"*Whatever* it takes. There's more than one way to bring down a zealot. I infused the poultice I used to pack his wound with the antidote for targul venom. It will counteract the tonic he takes to suppress his pheromone receptors for the next few days. He'll no longer be immune to your scent."

"And if he goes into a frenzy instead of spilling his secrets?"

Zwara shrugged. "I imagine it would cause quite a scandal. A high-ranking member of the Order breaking their sacred vow and attacking a queen. It would ruin their credibility." Zwara shot me a pointed look. "Make sure you have a witness."

My chin dipped in practiced obedience. I had no intention of inviting anyone to witness me end the zealot's life.

She dismissed me with a wave of her hand. "Go and let me bathe in peace."

I glanced over my shoulder as I left and watched Zwara relight one of the incense burners before dropping her robes and slipping into the pool.

⁓

"What do you mean he declined?" I glared at Niva through my veil.

"I'm sorry, Queen Vaza, but the commander refused to be escorted to your private chambers. He asked me to give you this." The priestess handed me a worn leather book.

I ran my fingers over the embossed title that had long since lost its luster. *Dangerous Creatures: A Medicinal Guide to the Use of Venom and Antidotes.*

Was it his way of telling me he knew Zwara had dosed him with anti-venom? *Fuck.* I flipped through the pages until I found the section on targuls, hoping there wasn't an antidote to the antidote. I'd gotten lucky the first time I'd stabbed him. He'd be impossible to kill without the distraction of my scent.

"He's waiting for us in the library."

I reined in my emotions before the anger flashed across my chest. "Of course. We'll meet wherever *the commander* is most comfortable." I gestured to the goblets of kelp wine and salted meats as I left the room. "Bring the refreshments when you come down."

The House of Blood's library sat at the base of the queen's keep tower and separated us from the rest of the sprawling castle below. It was the limit of where we could wander without an escort and where I spent most of my time when Zwara wasn't using my body to further her political power.

Before the current wave of red tides, fifty queens lived in the keep. Thirteen of us remained. Tesk and I were by far the youngest and the only two related by blood. With only us to look after, Hemeda had spoiled us terribly when we were young.

Zwara resented the attention she lavished on Tesk and me. As her apprentice, Zwara had a very different relationship with Hemeda. The elder priestess was cruel and relentless when it came to training blood mages and helped Zwara overcome her stunted gift. Our sister would never have become high priestess without Hemeda's harsh tutelage.

I wasn't sure what Zwara hated me for more—that I didn't have to work for the healer's affection or that I'd taken her mentor from her during my first mating rite. Hemeda insisted Zwara could never know the truth about what really happened.

I offered my thanks to the Nūkiri that Hemeda had made it out of the shack before the zealot tracked my scent straight to her. She'd hide in the catacombs until the wraith was able to return with a fresh supply of frenzy to rebuild our network of spies.

The way my spine was draining, I'd have at least a dozen vials by the next tide. I refused to give voice to the reason for it as I clutched the leather book in my hand. *Our business is just beginning, wraith.*

My silk pants hissed between my thighs, and I forced my steps to slow, annoyed that he was making me come to him. I ran a sweaty palm over my exposed hip and thigh where the crisscrossing gold cords held the fabric panels in place. The matching band around my breasts left the bioluminescent freckles across my chest on full display. It had taken years to master control of my light. I only wished the same could be said for the pheromones that gave entirely too much away.

The Keep's library smelled of mildew and salt. It was impossible to keep anything dry with the humidity and salty air. Some of the books were unreadable due to the mold. I found the zealot leaning out one of the high arched windows that lined the south wall. The view looked out over the House of Blood's dying gardens and the sea cliffs beyond.

"Plotting your escape, Commander?"

His leather armor creaked as he straightened. "Just ensuring the room is secure, my queen. The abundance of balconies and deep window moldings make the Keep easy to scale." He clenched the shaft of his spear, causing the muscles to tighten along the length of his bare arm.

"I can't imagine who would be capable of such a feat. You won't need your weapon here. I assure you, there are no dangerous creatures lurking behind the curtains or hiding in the shadows between shelves. Unless it's your intent to intimidate the priestesses. If that's the case, I'm afraid it will take more than a brooding glare and a pointy stick to strike fear in the hearts of Zwara's devotees."

His eyes dropped to the book clasped in my hands. "As you say, my queen."

If my scent had an impact on him, it didn't show. Zwara could have lied about the anti-venom to test me. I didn't trust her any more than I trusted the zealot.

"It was thoughtful of you to loan me something from the Rift's library while you interrogate the priestesses," I said, searching his face for a sign that he knew he'd been drugged. "I can't remember the last time I read something new. I've exhausted the tomes in the Keep's library."

"It's from my personal collection. I thought you might enjoy it, as we seem to have a common interest." The skin around his eyes crinkled with a smile. "I was a tracker for the House of Salt before I joined the Order."

Maybe he didn't know.

"Is that how you came by the scar? Hunting gorzin?"

"Prince Hazi and I joined together. I was bitten during our Ordeal."

I resisted the urge to roll my eyes beneath the veil. Recruits had three options to prove themselves worthy of taking vows to their dead deity. They could choose to show their bravery by sneaking into a gorzin nest and bringing back a fang. They could demonstrate their faith by spending a tide in silent vigil, blindfolded and on their knees on the steps of the temple and towering effigy of the god of tides without food or rest. Or they could volunteer to have their tongues removed in a permanent vow of silence to prove their loyalty after making the pilgrimage to the prophet's tomb.

"I don't understand why anyone would willingly subject themselves to torture."

"Spoken by one who bears the marks of her own ordeal." His brows knit together as he forced his eyes away from my scars. "If the Order was in control of the rites, queens would be free to choose their own mates and never be forced to perform in public rituals like slaves."

"Is that why you're here, Commander?" I waved a hand toward the opulent furnishings, rich fabrics, and beautifully carved bookshelves in the Keep's library with a soft laugh. "To free us from our bondage?

Trading one gilded cage for another isn't freedom. At least here, we're not indoctrinated with nonsense about ancient prophecies or forced to worship dead gods."

"I'm here," he said, gritting his teeth, "to find the drug dealer who calls herself the wraith and convince her to stop pumping uncut frenzy into the lower city. It's putting everyone's lives at risk, and it's my job to protect them."

"And it's my job to make sure you don't spread your doomsday rhetoric through the House of Blood." I kept my voice light.

"Have you ever even read the prophecy?"

"I'm not a fan of the sacrificial virgin trope."

Niva appeared and placed the tray of refreshments on a low table between two cushioned reading chairs built for queens, not wide shouldered warrior priests.

"Would you care for some wine before we start, Commander?" I asked.

"I'd prefer not to mix business with pleasure."

"How disappointing." I plucked a glass from the tray. "There are seven priestesses who serve the queens. I've arranged for you to meet with three today and the rest tomorrow. Niva will be your first interviewee. She attends to my sister and me and takes care of all our needs."

"Commander zurNaga." Niva bent her head in forced civility that did little to cover her disdain. I liked the mage and took no pleasure in treating her harshly. In another life, I liked to imagine we might even be friends. I sipped my wine through the sheer veil, drowning my guilt in its tangy sweetness. The killer queen had a reputation to uphold, and the wraith couldn't afford any more friends.

"Please, call me Brex." The zealot turned on the charm and flashed her a warm smile as he propped his spear against the closest bookshelf. "There's no need for formalities, priestess."

I moved to my usual spot on a parapet beneath one of the arched windows where the breeze would carry my scent throughout the room. Niva wouldn't notice. Like our female guards, all the queens' handmaids had their scent receptors removed.

"I have a few quick questions and promise not to take too much of your time." He sat first. The petite chair groaned under the weight of his massive body. He threw his arm casually over the back as if he owned the place.

Niva perched on the edge of the seat opposite him, back straight.

"Caring for two queens must keep you busy. I don't think I've ever seen you in attendance at any of the noble house balls."

No matter how hard I tried, I couldn't imagine him doing anything as frivolous as attending a ball.

"Those of us who care for the queens are quarantined to the temple, House of Blood, and connecting tunnels to ensure we don't contract the wasting and contaminate the water in their private baths."

"A wise precaution," he said. "With so few queens remaining, I'm glad to hear their health and safety remain a priority. Who chooses their guards?"

"The high priestess."

"And they're stationed at every entry point?"

"Yes. And at the door to each of the queen's private apartments and throughout the Keep." Niva gestured impatiently to the hall, where three female shield mages stood sentry. "As you've seen for yourself, Commander, the queens are quite safe here."

"Are the windows frequently left open?" He glanced to where I sat with the book I was pretending to read. I forced my eyes to the graphic illustration of a gorzin's open mouth dripping with deadly venom. Anyone who survived a gorzin bite was clearly favored by the god of tides who'd once commanded the sea serpents.

"Yes. Of course. The queens are kept as comfortable as possible. It would be stifling to breathe in here without the airflow."

"The high priestess must think very highly of you to entrust you with such an important job. Were you selected for the position, or did you have to apply?"

"The high priestess hand picks everyone assigned to attend the queens."

"Are you the only priestess permitted to collect frenzy from Queen Vaza and Queen Tesk?"

Niva lifted her chin. "I'm the only one allowed to touch them or to see them without their veils."

"Just you. No one else?"

The mage shifted in her seat. "Aside from the high priestess, of course."

"Of course." He flashed her another easy smile. "Does she ever attend to the queens?"

"She's far too busy overseeing the death rites. But Queen Vaza often attends to Tesk's comfort."

"Is that unusual?" he asked, leaning forward.

"For the other queens? Yes. But Tesk and Vaza are identical twins. They're very close," Niva said.

I turned the page I'd been staring at for too long as the zealot's curious gaze rolled over me. It was extremely rare for more than one queen to be born into the same pod.

"Where are the vials stored before and after you fill them with frenzy?" he asked after dragging his eyes back to Niva. "Can you walk me through the process?"

I loosened the sheer fabric around my face enough to be able to sip the sweet wine beneath my veil instead of through it. Niva explained how the recycled glass vials were sterilized, inventoried, and stored securely for health and safety reasons before use.

"Once they're filled," she said, "we hand deliver them to the high priestess. I'm not sure how she distributes them from there."

"Do you keep track of how many vials of frenzy you deliver to the high priestess?"

"No. I assume she keeps her own records."

"I'm sure she does. Has the high priestess ever mentioned visiting the catacombs beneath the city?"

I choked on my wine, sucking it down the wrong pipe and coughed uncontrollably.

Niva jumped up and came to assist, making even more of a scene. "Are you all right?"

"I'm fine." My voice came out hoarse as I shooed her away. "There was a bug in my glass. I accidentally swallowed it. Can you bring me some water?"

"Right away, Queen Vaza."

I stood and took a deep breath as I rubbed at the burning sensation in the center of my chest. How did he know about the catacombs? Had he tracked Hemeda there? Was she safe?

"I have one more question before you go, Niva." The mage hesitated at the doorway. "Are there any other priestesses in the House of Blood who possess the same unique shade of midnight blue hair as the high priestess?"

It had been dark. How had he seen my fucking hair?

"Blue hair?" Niva repeated.

"Zwara is the only one," I rasped. "Niva, the water, please." She dipped her head and left us.

The next two interviews went the same. I wandered the library where I could watch the zealot without being too obvious. He kept his body language open and relaxed the way he had with Niva as he asked his questions. Who oversaw security for the House of Blood? Who controlled access to frenzy? Who matched his description of the wraith?

They all gave the same answer. Zwara.

The high priestess was clearly his prime suspect. The wraith's true identity would be safe as long as the Order continued looking at my sister.

"Was your interrogation successful, Commander?" I asked when he came to find me after the last interview.

"It went as expected." He ran a hand through his unbound hair. I pretended not to notice the way his muscles flexed with the movement, but my body betrayed me. A bead of frenzy slid down my spine. His eyes darkened from peridot to deep moss, and I bit back a smile. The antidote was finally working.

"I could've told you what they'd say and saved us both an afternoon of boredom. Zwara wields power and cruelty in equal measure. Her disciples are too terrified to ever betray her."

He crossed his arms and leaned against the ornate bookcase. "You speak boldly for a queen."

"You mean for someone best seen and not heard? You'll have to forgive me for having an opinion about the tyrant who controls my life."

"On the contrary. I'm very interested in what you have to say on the subject. Perhaps I should have interviewed you instead."

"Ask your questions, Commander. I have no secrets."

A gentle buzzing sensation cascaded over my skin as he wrapped his shield around me, cocooning us in a bubble of silence.

"The high priestess provides the noble houses with a ration of frenzy from each queen. Why would she flood the lower city with only your scent?"

"You must be mistaken. The vial you brought Zwara was from another queen's spine, not mine. The differences are subtle, so it's understandable."

"I'm the best tracker in Eden. I don't make mistakes. The frenzy I gave the high priestess came from the House of Salt's ration. It has the same top notes as all the others, warm and slightly sweet. Your base notes are far more interesting. They smell like…"

Salt and sin. He closed his eyes and inhaled a deep breath through his nose. The memory of his body pressed against mine in the alley sent another drop of frenzy down the center of my back.

"Do tell, Commander. I'd love to know what I smell like to you." I took a step closer, daring him to repeat the words he'd said to me in the dark.

"Rage."

I halted in my tracks as he shoved off the wall and made a slow circle around me.

"I can smell everything you're feeling right now. Your desire is almost as potent as your fear. What are you afraid of, my queen? Getting caught?" I sucked in a breath as he lifted his fingers to my veiled lips. An almost touch. "I know the high priestess drugged me and ordered you to seduce me."

"Is it working?" I asked.

A low growl rumbled through his chest. "I've imagined getting on my knees and claiming your pleasure against these shelves until you whimper my name." Light pulsed from my chest as he backed away from me with a cocky smile. "Is that what you wanted to hear?"

"Bold words for a zealot," I said, unsure of what I hated more, the way the image he painted made my insides go molten or how he'd used it to outmaneuver me.

A buzzing sensation kissed my skin as he released his shield.

"Tell the high priestess she'll need to be more creative if she wants to break me." He dipped his head and left me standing there, soaked in my own frenzy.

CHAPTER FIVE

RENAE

"LIAM RILEY, SINCE WHEN do you like to run?" I braided my hair with my back to the bathroom mirror, not needing a reminder of my corpse-like appearance, even though this bleached-out version of me was an upgrade from the charred form my death shade had taken after my first life.

"I don't," Liam called from the kitchen, "but I've missed seeing that incredible ass of yours bounce from behind."

I glanced back and squeezed my flat butt cheek, hoping he was prepared to be disappointed. There wasn't enough meat left on my rear to grab hold of, much less bounce. Liam did his best to cover the foul flavor that permeated our food and everything else here. I forced myself to eat and to run, but my body still refused to heal.

I secured my braid with a bread tie I'd found in the kitchen and inspected the bruises—yellow, purple, and red bleeding into one another like ink blots on a blinding white canvas. Liam tried to hide his concern, but the emotion seeped out of him like sweat. I tasted it on my tongue, salty and metallic, every time he studied me in his intense, probing way.

"Would you deny a man his one and only guilty pleasure?" His eyes flicked to mine as he leaned against the doorway, arms crossed.

"You have more than one guilty pleasure, my love."

The man couldn't help eavesdropping on my thoughts despite his best effort to block them. I'd resorted to burying the worst of my inner monologue beneath an old memory of my father to keep them private. The physical act of weaving that ridiculous rope and building the basket traps helped tie the memories together and solidify the camouflage. He'd freak out and lock me in the house indefinitely if he knew about the excursions I'd been making to create a map of the island while he was in his studio. If I could find a way out—something he missed—we could get out of this living hell before we ran out of time.

"True, but most of my guilty pleasures revolve around your ass." Liam pulled me closer and gripped my dwindling backside through the loose boxers I wore. "We should skip the run."

"We can't lounge about and have sex all day, every day for eternity."

"Agree to disagree." He dropped his head and traced the column of my throat with his lips as he backed me against the sink.

My gift raced beneath my skin with the need to latch on and drink him in. I withheld my psychic syphons despite the overwhelming urge to let them lick over him. The sulfuric aftertaste fouled everything here, including Liam's energy. Especially on the days when he locked himself up in his studio for hours. He always came back tasting like regret and rotten eggs. The thought of tasting it on him now made my stomach revolt, even as heat pooled between my thighs. I dug my nails into his back as he pressed kisses into my clavicle and bare shoulders. Liam cupped my breast and dropped his mouth to my nipple, rolling it between his teeth and tongue through the T-shirt I'd tied around my chest.

He'd been gentle with me so far, holding back because of my bruises and treating me like one of his delicate sculptures. "Harder." I fisted his hair and pulled him closer. "I'm not made of glass. I won't shatter."

Liam jerked his head away from my grip and nipped at my ear. "Is that a challenge? Because I know for a fact that I can make you shatter at least three times before you're spent. I'm happy to help you unlock a new record."

My body flushed with a cold sweat as he lifted me to the counter.

"No." I immediately scrambled away from his embrace as the memory of him screaming and clutching his skull the one and only time we'd had sex in a bathroom flashed through my head.

Liam winced, reading the memory of him collapsing after the aneurysm that sent his brain into a coma and his soul into the Void.

"Fuck. I wasn't thinking. I'm sorry." He kissed my temple and ushered me out of the too-small room. "I think we could both use some fresh air. Let's go for that run."

⁊

Each breath was like breathing underwater. The island wore humidity like a wool coat, damp and heavy against my skin. I tried to remind myself that none of this was real. Not the island. Not the ocean. Not the sun-bronzed god running next to me and barely breaking a sweat. The pulse screaming in my ears as my feet sank into sugar-soft sand said otherwise. My real husk was in a stasis tank hidden in the bowels of a greenhouse in Hawaii. Liam's was waiting for him in an ICU hospital bed. These husks we were dragging around the island were something else entirely. Something I hadn't worked out yet. According to Liam, the Void existed outside the laws of physics that governed the living and the dead.

Here, we were neither.

The intense midday sun dried the sweat from my skin. Liam's long, easy strides outpaced me as we raced down the beach. Ten years of hard living had honed his already sinuous lines into sculpted marble. Gods, he was beautiful to watch, even if it was all an illusion.

We were alone on this island, but we weren't the only souls imprisoned in the Void. I'd sensed others—too many to count—after I was sucked into the Astral and Ziggy's psychic GPS sent me hurtling through the space between worlds. I'd swerved and twisted around the crystalized debris of souls that had long hardened and gone dim and slammed into faceted structures that left my body broken and bruised. Liam's glowing consciousness was firm when I crashed into it, yet still pliable enough to wrap around me like taffy and pull me in with him. I tried not to think about the dark crystals, the ones with no light left inside.

Was that what was to become of us?

Time moved faster in the Void. Ten years here for Liam had only been a few days for me in the city of the dead. Two days. That's all it had taken to gum up Liam's energy. How much longer did he have before it hardened completely?

I didn't know how much time we had left, but I was sure about one thing. Something was depleting energy from the imprisoned souls—something that tasted like rotten eggs.

Nausea oozed in my stomach. I slowed to a jog and fought the urge to double over and vomit in the sand. My brief swim through the Void had taken a heavy toll on my energy. That oily fluid had absorbed as much of me as it could.

"How are you not even winded?" I asked as my head spun. I'd pushed too hard trying to keep up with him.

The molten cocky smile died on his lips as he jogged back to where I'd stopped to ease my heaving chest. Liam scooped me up and carried me toward the shade of the tree line.

The world spun as I squirmed in his arms. "Put me down. I'm perfectly capable of walking."

His grip tightened around me. "Not a chance. You need to cool down and rest before you pass out from heat stroke. When was the last time you drank any water?"

My head throbbed with a dry, sucking pain. I stopped struggling and let him play protector because I was too stubborn to admit that it had been a few days since I'd forced myself to drink the sulfur-infused swill that came out of the kitchen tap.

A too-warm wind knocked palm fronds together as the sky darkened and a light rain wet my skin. Liam didn't slow down or stop when we reached the trees.

"Where are we going?" My voice came out hoarse and scratchy.

"To a freshwater lagoon. You're dehydrated, and it's closer than the bungalow."

The inside of my throat scraped together as I swallowed, unable to form any more words. I tried to get my bearings as he followed an invisible path through the rainforest so I could find the path again later. He'd never mentioned the lagoon before, and my curiosity went to war with the weight of my eyelids. Exhaustion won.

☙

The rancid scent of rotten eggs stuffed up my nose as Liam jostled me awake. We sat in a shallow pool of the bluest water I'd ever seen. He'd propped me against a tangle of cypress roots.

"Drink this." Liam held a leafy cone-shaped cup to my mouth.

I gagged and swatted his hands away as the liquid slid down my throat. "Gods, what is that?"

"Water. Now take another sip." He lifted the cup to my lips with shaking hands.

I turned away. "Why does it smell and taste like a toilet?"

"It's from an underground spring. The smell isn't that bad. Hold your breath and chug it." I did as instructed and let him tip the contents into my mouth but couldn't make myself swallow. Water trickled from my lips as I fought the urge to dry heave.

"This is why I don't want you going for runs on your own. You're not indestructible anymore, and that wicked stubborn streak of yours is going to get you killed." Liam scooped me up and strode into the lagoon until he was chest deep and my body floated in his arms. "Wet your head."

He loosened his grip enough for me to tip my head back into the water. My first thought was of how long it would take to wash the stink from my hair. Then I noticed the smell had disappeared.

"Did you cast a projection to cover the smell?"

Liam set me on my feet. "I'm blocking the sulfuric smell and taste with a shield."

"If you're an isolator like Lucy, why haven't you compelled me to eat?"

"Trust me, I've tried. I don't think I got that part of the gift my father and his research partner shoved inside me."

"Or maybe it just doesn't work on me? We won't know for sure unless we get out of here."

The scar that cut across his forehead deepened as he scowled down at me. "You need to drink."

I cupped the cool water in my palms and gulped greedily until my stomach sloshed. "I'm feeling better. Are you happy now?" I asked as I stepped back and splashed water at his sour face.

Liam gripped my elbow as my feet slipped on the algae-covered rocks. "Careful, we're close to the edge."

I peered down into a funnel-shaped hole beneath the surface. The water was crystal clear and so deep I couldn't see the bottom. "What is it?"

"The ass crack of the island, if I had to guess."

I pushed away from him and swam over the cave-like structure. It did kind of resemble a giant orifice half a dozen feet below the surface. It was at least twenty feet wide at its mouth, then narrowed as it deepened. The rock walls were studded with little crystals that sparkled in the sun.

I dove under to get a better look and felt Liam's overprotective anxiety surge along the bond as he tugged the invisible cord back toward him.

I kicked back to the surface and flipped onto my back. "It's beautiful."

With Liam blocking the off-putting smell, the lagoon was incredible. Dappled sunlight danced on the water. Golden limestone rocks warmed by the sun beckoned to be sprawled upon. Flowering vines hung from trees and trailed the water's edge, dropping white petals on the glass-like surface.

I righted myself to get a better look at the spot where the impenetrable wall of woven trees and vines that surrounded the lagoon had been peeled back like a curtain.

"Have you been hiding this from me?"

Liam raked a hand through his hair and waded to a dry rock to sit. "I wasn't hiding it from you. I was just... being cautious." He gestured to the bottomless hole beneath me. "When I shift my vision, I can see the energy ley lines. They all extend outward from here. Everything on the island is a pieced-together approximation of places I was familiar with in the real world. The white sand beaches, my bungalow, the rainforest behind it. But I've never seen a geological formation like this. I don't know how it got here, but it's clearly the beating heart of this island."

My skin prickled as I climbed out of the water to sit next to him. "Have you tried diving to the bottom?"

"Once." The scar between his eyes puckered.

"And?"

"I ran out of air." Liam angled toward me and cupped my cheek. "Promise me you won't try to swim down there. It's not safe."

"I'm a good swimmer."

"You used to be able to run flat out for forty miles through the woods in the middle of a thunderstorm with no shoes to spy on me. Yet five miles on the beach here did you in. Things change. You're not superhuman anymore, chica. You need to listen to what your body is telling you. You're getting weaker by the day. The little bit you've been eating isn't enough."

"The salmon and peas taste like sulfur. I can barely stomach them."

"Then feed on me. Siphon my energy like before when I was struggling to control it."

Silt squished between my toes as I waded to shore. Liam stood from his rock and followed. How could I tell him the thought of tasting the island on him made my insides roll? But I didn't need to *tell* him. He'd already read the thought.

Liam wrapped his arms around my waist from behind. "I know the vileness of this place has seeped into my veins and tainted the way my energy tastes, but you still need to feed. You haven't used your syphons on me since the night we completed the bond. I can project any flavor you want." He brushed his lips over the shell of my ear. "What are you craving, chica?"

What I really wanted was for him to taste like he used to—the milky sweet heat of bourbon and cream that warmed my chest and reminded me of home. But I couldn't ask a recovered alcoholic and addict to project that into my brain.

I wound my fingers through his and brought his palm to my throat. "Marshmallows. Big fluffy marshmallows. And I want you to stop treating me like I'm going to break. Claim me like you did on the sea cliffs, and I'll feed as often as you like."

He twisted me in his arms. "Are you seriously trying to bargain with me over your own damn health? Play rough or watch you waste away?"

"If it gets you to stop acting like an overprotective ass, yes."

"Fine." The word came out like a guttural growl as he backed me against a tree and pinned me in place with his rigid body.

He pressed his lips to mine in a kiss that was hard and demanding. Rough bark scraped my skin, sending a flood of heat through my core. A tingling sensation followed his hands as they ran along the underside of my arms, lifting them above my head. He held them high above me with one hand, letting his other slide down to bracket my throat.

"Is this what you want?" Something cool and smooth snaked around my wrists, tugging them higher.

I glanced up as the vine tightened around my wrists and bound me to a branch. "I want all of you inside all of me." I bit back a smile as two more vines coiled around my ankles.

"Oh, I am 100 percent going to fuck you against this tree, but not until you release your syphons and take your fill from me like a good little reaper."

Something that might have been an angry curse or a desperate moan tumbled out of me as Liam pressed closer, grinding his thigh against my throbbing center.

Heat crept up my neck as I gritted my teeth and growled at him. "That's not what I meant when I asked you to claim me."

Liam hooked a finger under my chin and forced me to look at him as desire and determination pulsed along the bond between us. His voice came out soft when he finally spoke.

"I know exactly what you meant, but my gifts have advanced since the last time I poured my power into you and took control of your syphons. I'm not gonna do that while you're in this condition. I just got you back. I won't lose you again, Renae. If that means I need to act like an overprotective ass to keep you from starving to death, then I will. You have two choices. You can stop being a stubborn brat and feed on me right now." He teased my lips open. "Or you can squirm while I torture you with my tongue until you're so desperate to come that you concede."

"What makes you think I'll concede?"

"Because you have an insatiable appetite, and you're already starving." Heat licked through my core as he took a step back and raked his eyes over my body.

I bit back a smile. "Then I choose torture."

"I was hoping you'd say that." Liam closed the distance between us and traced my cracked lips with his finger. "I've waited ten years to feel you feed on me while we fuck. I can hold out a little longer while I worship your flesh. How long will you last before you beg me to push you over the edge?"

"I don't need your help to have an orgasm."

"No, but you do need your hands." The vine binding my wrists tightened as Liam inspected the old T-shirt I'd used to bind my breasts. He tugged at the knot and unwound me. I closed my eyes, waiting for his hands and the heat of his mouth. A cool breeze licked my bare skin, sending a cascade of gooseflesh over my body. My nipples prickled to attention, but Liam didn't touch me.

My eyes popped open at the ripping of fabric. "Hey, that's my only shirt."

"I have three more in decent condition back at the house. What's mine is yours. Tip your head forward." His warm salt-and-sweat scent engulfed me as I leaned forward and let him tie the torn strip over my eyes.

Liam lifted my chin and pressed his lips to mine, teasing my mouth open with his tongue. It was deep and gentle and laced with restrained need. I knew he was holding back because he loved me and was afraid to hurt me. But I needed it to hurt—just a little—to make it feel real. Pain had always been my anchor. The one uncompromising thing reminding me that I was alive.

"I'm all in for making it a game. If you need me to stop or unbind you, all you have to do is think it. But if you want me to get you off, you'll have to syphon me first."

I arched my back and brushed my nipples against his chest. "I understand."

"So eager." Liam pressed a palm against my belly, pushing me against the tree. "You're already squirming, and I haven't even gotten started."

He slid his hands up and down my sides and over my arms to the branch above my head. "You can grab this for support."

I curled my fingers around the wood, gripping tightly, and gasped as he kicked my feet apart. He silenced my surprise with his mouth, kissing me hard and deep as he palmed me between my thighs.

When I kissed him back, he pulled away but kept a reassuring hand on me. All I could see through the blindfold was the play of light and shadow as he traced the contours of my body with his fingertips.

"I didn't think you could get any more beautiful when you looked like sin and fire, but I was wrong. Now you look like a goddess." He brushed his knuckles over the underside of my breasts.

Liam's stubble scraped over my ribs. He blazed a trail with his tongue and soothed it with little gusts of air. My syphons throbbed hot beneath my skin, aching to be released as he slid his hands over my hips and pushed the wet boxers down my legs. I angled my head and neck in an attempt to peek under the bottom of the blindfold.

"No cheating, chica."

"No squirming. No peeking. No touching. How many more rules does this game have?"

Liam pressed a kiss to my belly as he pushed my knees apart and settled between them.

"You can touch me," he said, his breath tickling the soft mound of hair above my pussy, "but only with your syphons."

He pressed a kiss to my inner thigh as he traced my wet seam with a gentle touch. I moaned as his fingers and tongue played follow the leader, caressing and teasing me everywhere except where I wanted it most. Warmth spread from my core as he pushed two fingers inside me.

I arched against him as he pumped in and out with long, lingering strokes. He pulled my wetness through the folds and circled my clit, alternating between light touches and little licks. Gods, this man knew exactly what to do to make me whimper and beg.

Liam sealed his open mouth over me and slowly sucked, creating a vacuum-like pressure. I pulled at my restraints, needing to get a hand free to fist his hair. He hummed against me as the vines tightened around my wrists.

He unsealed his mouth and blew little puffs of air against my engorged flesh. I was so close to the edge I almost came as he flattened his tongue over my clit.

Then he was gone. Cool air rushed in where he'd been, the way it licked and curled around me an exquisite extension of his touch against my heated flesh. My heart pounded as I uncoiled my syphons from my back and swept the empty space in front of me, searching for him.

I didn't even try to hide the panic that crept into my voice when I called his name.

"Over here."

He was standing to my left, just out of my reach. But he knew that. His altered sight allowed him to see the six psychic appendages I used to read emotions and suck energy from my unknowing victims.

"You're fucking beautiful," he said.

"Come closer."

"Are you ready to concede?"

Gods, yes.

My syphons latched on to him as he erased the distance between us. His erection rested heavy against my hip, and the heat of his naked body chased the chill from my skin. Sweet, sugary bliss laced my tongue as I drank him in and my syphons explored all the places I wanted and needed to touch.

"That's my girl." Liam's lips grazed my ear as he swept two fingers through the wetness between my legs and brought them to my mouth. "I want you to taste what I taste when I feast on you."

My lips parted, and he pressed his fingers inside, spreading the salty tang of my essence over my tongue where it mingled with the marshmallowy bliss he'd projected to flavor his energy. It wasn't the intoxicating, sweet milky heat I craved, but it was enough to make me want to gorge myself on him.

"See? Not everything here is contaminated. You, my ravenous reaper, taste as exquisite as ever."

He pressed his knee between my legs. I buried all six barbed syphons deep inside him. He groaned and braced a hand against the tree above my head. His other arm circled around my waist and tugged me higher on his leg. Still slick with desire, I rocked my hips and rode his muscular thigh as I took my fill. There was no trace of sulfur or the contaminating effects of the island. It was just Liam and me.

Need settled like an aching heaviness between my hips. The vines retreated from my wrists and ankles, and I used the branch for leverage as I wrapped my legs around him. He pulled the head of his cock through my wet folds before slowly pressing into me, inch by inch, as I stretched around him.

"Fuck." He moaned as I coiled my syphons around his shoulders, back, and legs, piercing his aura and burrowing deep as I pulled him closer.

Rough tree bark bit my back as he nailed me against it. Our bodies became a frantic tangle of limbs and syphons, moving faster and harder as if neither of us could get deep enough or satisfy the need to climb inside one another. I clung to him as the orgasm ripped through me like lightning. Static crackled over our bodies as Liam grabbed my ass and unloaded inside me.

That's when the visions came—burning palms over hot glass, the hair-raising tingle of lightning, the prick of a needle, followed by a warm rush in my veins, then complete and utter euphoria. Everything he'd done before I arrived. Things he was still doing.

I ripped the blindfold off my eyes, unable to stop the surge of fear and disappointment that took turns pulsing through me. He was using again.

"Why?"

Liam's forehead dipped to mine. "I'm sorry. I didn't mean for you to see that. I forgot about your erratic visions." He flattened a palm between my breasts as if he were desperate to measure every heartbeat between us. "It was too hard to be here without you."

I brought my hands to his face and cupped his cheeks, too many thoughts and emotions swirling inside me to form words.

"It still feels like I can't quite take a deep breath unless we're this close and I'm sheathed inside you."

I didn't want to imagine what his life must have been like while he lived alone for so long. Hot tears streaked down my cheeks as I tried to drop my legs. "It's my fault. If I'd gotten here sooner..."

He tightened his grip and kept me sealed against him. He was still sheathed between my thighs, unwilling to break the connection, like it was some kind of tether. Like I'd disappear if he let me go.

"No, chica, don't blame yourself. This is entirely on me. This island has a way of getting inside your head and destroying you from the inside out. I knew what I was doing when I accepted defeat." His denim blue eyes went glassy. "I broke the promise I made to you once. No more secrets. No more lies. I should have told you that I was using the moment you arrived."

I had no idea what to say. How to be supportive and understanding without passing judgment, even though it nagged at my chest. "How often?"

"Twice a day, just to stay ahead of the withdrawal symptoms."

The glass studio he hadn't invited me to see. It was the only time he let me out of his sight.

"Do you want to stop?"

He didn't answer right away. "Maybe. I don't know. Detox is a bitch. I won't be able to keep the offshore storm away or protect you if I'm sick."

There would be no convincing him that I didn't need protection after I'd collapse this afternoon. I swept my thumbs over his damp cheeks. "Tell me what I can do to help."

"Don't give up on me." Liam kissed me like it was a question.

I kissed him back. Deep and slow like it was a promise. A promise to get him off this island before it destroyed us both.

Chapter Six

VAZA

"It reeks in here." Tesk threw the windows of my sleep chamber open. The frenzy-soaked sheet clung to my damp skin as I pulled it over my head to block the light.

"What time is it?" I flinched as my swollen spine pressed into the mattress.

"Time for you to take a bath. You smell like sour kelp. How much did you drink last night?"

"Not enough, apparently."

"There are worse things than being in heat," she said sarcastically. "I don't think I've ever seen your scent glands weep this much."

"It's this stifling room. I must have sweated it out."

"Are you sure it doesn't have something to do with the ruggedly handsome male you spent all afternoon flirting with."

"He's not handsome. He's a zealot, and I was absolutely not flirting with him."

"That's not what the other queens said. Heleena told Giza that you let him charm you into a frenzy."

"Brex zurNaga is about as charming as a gorzin, and the other queens are vapid busybodies who need to mind their own business." I yanked my feet out of the way as Tesk flopped onto the foot of my bed. She looked even worse than I felt. She was no doubt still exhausted from the discomfort and restlessness caused by her first heat.

"Can you blame them? It's not like there's anything else to talk about in this place. Let them have their fun."

My gaze landed on the leather-bound book in her hands. "What are you reading?" I asked, eager to change the subject.

"Oh, you know, just a little uplifting tale about disease, famine, and food chain collapse." Tesk tried to dismiss the nervous waver in her voice with a flick of her wrist.

I snatched the book from her and read the title. *The Seven Signs of the End of Tides.* "Where did you get this garbage?"

"Niva brought it up while you were sleeping. She told me to tell you the not-at-all charming or attractive eel is waiting for you in the library."

"He's here?" After our last conversation, I'd assumed he wouldn't show up for the remainder of the interviews and that I'd lost my only opportunity to end him. I swung my feet to the floor and padded across the room to my closet.

"Niva said he's looking for a frenzy thief who calls herself the wraith."

"He's interviewing priestesses with direct access to the drug," I said as I shoved my legs into a pair of leggings and pulled on a tunic that would hide my engorged spine.

"What does that have to do with you? And don't you dare tell me it's better if I don't know."

I cut her a sidelong glance as I twisted my hair into a tight knot. "Zwara ordered me to get close to him and find out what he knows."

Tesk heaved a sigh. "I'd say he knows quite a bit." She picked up the book and handed it to me. "You need to read the inscription."

I flipped to the first page. *Hello, wraith. If you want me to keep your secret, meet me tonight where survivors do their duty to the dead.*

"Did Niva see this?" I asked, surprised by the steadiness of my voice.

Tesk shook her head. "I don't think so. It came in a box."

"Show me." I followed my sister into the main chamber. My stomach rolled as the remnants of the previous night's bad decisions pressed up my throat. The box that hid my secret stash of frenzy in the catacombs sat on a low table between tufted floor cushions and empty bottles of wine.

"He has Hemeda," I said.

"Hemeda? What's she got to do with this?" Tesk asked. "Is that who you've been sneaking out to meet? Please tell me you're not this drug dealer the Order is searching for."

"I should have killed him the first time we met," I said as I searched frantically for my veil.

Tesk grabbed my shoulders. "Stop. What kind of trouble have you gotten yourself into?"

"The less you know, the better. Let me go. I need to deal with the zealot."

"No. I'm tired of being lied to because you don't think I can handle the truth. When we were young and bullied by Zwara, you told me I was the only one in this world you trusted. When did that change?" A tear slipped down her pallid cheek.

"This world is brutal and unforgiving, Tesk. I'm trying to protect you from the worst of it."

She took the book from me. "According to this, I'm supposed to sacrifice myself to the god of tides. If that's truly my fate, there's nothing you can do to stop the worst from coming for me."

"It's alarmist propaganda, nothing more." I was so going to gut that hulking pile of trench sludge for filling Tesk's head with unfounded fears.

"What if it's not? All the signs foretold by the prophecy are happening. The return of the red tide. Food shortages and famine."

"This isn't the first cursed tide, and it won't be the last." I smoothed my palm over her silken hair.

"This is the longest one we've ever had. I don't know how much more I can take, Vaz. What if it's true? What if I am the *ki'sikilta*?" Tears silvered the corners of her eyes.

My markings lit beneath my tunic. The blue-green glow cast Tesk's face in a sickly light. "Don't speak that word aloud. Don't even think it. You are not their *ki'sikilta*. I will *never* let them take you."

Her gills flared with fear. That's when I smelled it. There was no mistaking the sharp tang of pus that came with the onset of the wasting. I pressed the back of my hand to her forehead.

"You're burning up," I said.

She swatted my hand away. "I feel fine. It's just this heat." Her eyelids fluttered shut as she swayed on her feet. I wrapped my arm around her waist and guided her into the bathing chamber.

"You'll be more comfortable once you cool down." I struggled to keep my voice calm as I helped her into the tub, shift and all. Once it crossed from the gills to the lungs, the wasting was fatal. The only way to stop it from advancing was to freeze her gills or cauterize them with magic the way Hemeda had done to mine. There wasn't enough time to hunt down an ice mage or summon a priestess. By the time they got here, it would be too late.

I whispered a desperate offering to the god of tides and anyone else who might be listening as I knelt beside her. Asking for forgiveness for what I was about to do and offering him my life in exchange for hers.

After they were dethroned, the Order of Wu'uru declared the consumption of a soul the most heinous crime in Kateri law. Punishable by cruciation—the full removal of a queen's reproductive organs.

According to the old texts, reviving a soul and stealing its power was a dangerous practice. The awakened entity could take over and devour you instead. The Nūkiri were the only ones who'd ever been strong enough to survive the process.

None of that mattered.

I dug my claws into the floor as my mind retreated into the tomb at my core. The sacred space where my mind retreated during the rite and the souls of the dead enveloped me in their energy until it was over.

I pushed deeper, letting the memory of all those diseased corpses on the body carts drive me into the well of souls I carried inside me. That would not be Tesk's fate.

There were so many buzzing gossamer threads. They surrounded me like the tide, pushing against me and pulling me under all at once. I let the gentle hum envelop me as I searched for the high-pitched vibration that marked the frequency of an ice mage.

I grasped a glowing blue strand and thrust for the surface of my consciousness. I had no idea if it would work or if I'd survive long enough to save my sister.

My vision exploded with blinding color as the mage awoke inside me. Pain cracked through my skull as their memories and magic settled into the crevices of my brain, filling every available space with noise.

I doubled over, screaming in pain as I grasped my head and prayed for the chaos to settle. But the voice coming out of my mouth wasn't mine. Someone else was in control.

"Where am I?" it said, and I felt my head rotate as it took in my chambers—the silk sheets and unmade bed, the elegant arched window and billowing curtains.

My stomach rolled as whoever was seeing through my eyes glanced down at the silver scars covering my chest and arms. "I'm not supposed to be here. I... I died."

Water sloshed into my lap as Tesk grasped my arm, forcing me—us—to look at her. "Vaza?"

"My name is Pila," the voice whimpered as our gaze lifted to Tesk. I was vaguely aware of the guards breaking into the main chamber of my apartment.

My sister's lips curled back, revealing her flesh-shredding fangs. "You fucking slug slut. What have you done?"

Pila cowered away, allowing my consciousness to surge forward. Tesk's hooked claws ripped through my forearm as I jerked away from her to the wet floor, a single thought in my head. *Ice. I need ice. Now.*

Pain prickled down my arms. Each exhaled breath crystallized in midair. The puddle beneath my hands froze and cracked as the cold spread from my palms, across the floor and up the walls, coating everything in a glistening sheet of ice. Snowflakes materialized and fluttered to the slick floor as the blue ceiling thickened and turned white.

"She's been possessed," someone yelled. "Seize her."

A blade whizzed through the air. I lifted my arms to protect Tesk, and the water rose from the tub and solidified into a wall of ice, bisecting the room, trapping the guards on the opposite side. Warmth spread across my belly. I glanced down at the hilt of a dagger protruding from my abdomen. My only thought as I pulled it out was that I needed to freeze the wasting from Tesk's lungs before I died.

She choked on a sob as she climbed out of the tub and pressed her hands to the wound on my stomach. I gripped her wrists. Frost crept up her arms, slower this time. The power was waning, fizzling out.

"Vaza, please. Don't do this. Put the soul back." Tesk's plea turned into a pained cry as the ice crept inside her gills.

"I'm sorry. It's the only way to stop the wasting," I said through chattering teeth.

It wasn't until her rasping breaths transformed into a deep inhale that I allowed myself to pull back and breathe. The air around her was thick with the metallic mix of iron and ice and not a trace of the wasting.

The barbed hooks in my brain eased, and the chaos quieted. Pila was gone. Used up.

"Thank you," I whispered, vaguely aware of the guards' muffled shouts mingling with a familiar deep voice on the other side of the wall.

A searing cramp ripped through my abdomen as I pressed my hands over Tesk's where they'd frozen to my belly. Warm blood squelched through our fingers, breaking the bond.

"Do whatever it takes to survive." The voice that came out of me was a hoarse whisper and all my own. My head felt too heavy and weightless all at once.

"Don't you dare leave me, Vaza."

The whine of cleaving ice split the air. My eyes squeezed shut, unable to hold back the weight of exhaustion that clamped down around me as I toppled sideways.

Someone hauled me up off the floor. The last thing I remember was the deep voice that shook the room.

"Whoever threw that knife better fucking run."

Chapter Seven
VAZA

I ARCHED OFF THE stone slab as searing pain ripped through my abdomen.

"Everyone out," Zwara hissed. "I don't work in front of an audience."

A buzzing sensation kissed my skin, and the pain evaporated.

"No silver. She has enough reminders of what's been taken from her. I'll not let you give her another."

My head rolled to the side, and I met the god of tides' jeweled-glass eyes. A blurred figure stood in front of the windows. I closed my eyes for what could have been a moment or maybe hours.

Muffled voices floated around me as I drifted in and out of consciousness.

"Will she live?"

"Vaza is too stubborn to die, but she'll never be able to spawn again. The damage is irreversible. I had to cauterize the wound to stop the bleeding since you wouldn't let me silver it."

I sank into the deepest part of myself. My mind spun as I fell, faster and faster, twisting and grasping for purchase where there was none. No vibrating threads to reach for. No cushion of souls to break my fall. I crashed into the bottom of my empty clutch.

A chasm opened inside me like the maw of a gorzin ready to swallow me whole. I kicked and screamed and clawed my way back to the surface, away from my hollowed-out core as the ache of that yawning emptiness settled into my bones.

Zwara may have saved me from dying, but she'd also taken away my gift. The only magic I owned. She'd taken the one thing I truly cared about away from me, aside from Tesk.

Fog filled my head as I fought to open my eyes, pushing back against the shield mage compelling me to remain immobilized.

"Your quick thinking saved her life. Take her back to the Keep. She'll remain under guard while she recovers and I decide what to do with her."

"As you say, your highness." I felt my limp body float toward the ceiling. "Sleep."

His voice washed through me like sedative tonic, and I had no choice but to comply with the whispered command.

***

Nightmares plagued my sleep. I couldn't stop seeing Tesk's and Hemeda's lifeless faces. One covered in blood, the other frozen behind a wall of ice. They twisted together. Tesk was the victim of my attack during my first mating rite while Hemeda was sacrificed by the zealot. No matter how hard I tried, I couldn't save either of them.

Someone screamed in the next room, jolting me awake, and I felt the vibration in my chest. Or maybe it was me. I couldn't be sure what was real and what was in my head.

"Why is she still shaking?"

"She's in shock." The deep voice at my side was less garbled than the others. "Bring me another blanket. We need to keep her warm."

"We need to send her back to the high priestess. Better to let her die on Zwara's watch so she can't accuse the Order of forcing the prophecy."

"She was gutted by one of her own guards. I'm not sending her anywhere until I can guarantee her safety."

"You killed a guard and abducted a queen. There will be consequences."

Chair legs scraped against stone. "She sacrificed herself to save the *ki'sikilta* and almost died in my arms. She's under my protection now."

"At least let someone else keep watch. You've barely slept in the last three days."

I groaned as I rolled onto my side, teeth chattering.

"Leave us and don't come back until you've secured the deal."

A door opened and shut.

Something big and warm curled around me from behind.

"Keep fighting, my queen. I'm not finished with you yet."

The darkness closed in again, and this time, I let it consume me.

❧

The stench of blood and brine and rotting flesh shoved up my nose. There was only one place that could claim such a level of rank perfume. The caves beneath the catacombs, where even the dead dared not linger.

Bile pressed at the back of my throat as it all came rushing back.

The ice.

The knife.

The deal I'd made with my enemy's dead god.

Fire licked across my stomach as I sat up in the middle of the creaking cot. I pulled up the oversized tunic that definitely didn't belong to me and inspected the thick rope of scar tissue on my abdomen.

She'll never be able to spawn again.

The punishment for stealing a soul was a full cruciation—the removal of a queen's clutch and reproductive organs. But Zwara didn't need to cruciate me. The guard's knife had seen to that. There would be no more rites. No more doing my duty to the dead after being sold to the highest bidder. A tickle started in my throat and grew into a deranged laugh and then a pained growl as the bruised muscles in my stomach pulled taut.

Someone cleared their throat, and I cut my eyes to the table in the corner of the room. The shirtless commander of the Order Guard sat in a too-small chair, reading a book, legs stretched out in front of him.

"Welcome back, *wraith*. The soreness will improve as soon as you get up and start moving around," he said without looking up.

Spiked shackles hung from one of the walls, and I tried not to imagine what he'd done to Hemeda to get her to give up my identity. He hadn't taken me to the Rift, which told me that either the Order didn't know he was holding me hostage or he had plans for me they wouldn't condone.

"Are you going to torture me?" My voice came out hoarse.

"Don't tempt me with a good time." He used his foot to nudge the extra chair out from the table. "Come eat."

My stomach growled as if on cue, and I hated that he knew what my body needed before I did. My every muscle ached as I dropped my feet to the cold floor and stood on wobbly legs. The embroidered silver hem of the huge tunic brushed my knees as I crossed the room.

He poured water into a goblet and placed it in front of me as I sat down.

"Where are my clothes?"

He slid a plate of dried meat toward me. "Information doesn't come free, and I require payment in advance." The corner of his mouth twitched as he repeated my words from our first encounter in the alley. "I'll answer a question for every bite you take."

"You need to practice your negotiation skills, zealot. You just offered me both things I desire. Answers and a full belly." I picked up one of the blackened squares of meat and popped it into my mouth. I gagged at the wretched flavor and immediately spit it back out. "What is that?"

I drained my goblet to wash away the rancid metallic taste lingering on my tongue.

"Aged whale liver. It was considered a delicacy in ancient Eden. It's high in iron and will help you heal. You lost a lot of blood. Next question."

"That didn't count. I didn't mean to ask that."

"Maybe you should practice your negotiation skills."

I wanted to fling the plate at his head. But I was starving, and I needed him to tell me where he was holding Hemeda, so I bit back my response and choked down a small cube.

"Am I a prisoner?"

"No."

I swallowed the next piece without chewing.

"Am I free to leave?"

"Not until I'm satisfied with the negotiations for your return." He eyed me as he refilled my water. "It helps if you don't breathe through your nose when you chew."

"So, I'm a hostage?"

"You're my guest."

"Is Hemeda also a *guest* in your secret dungeon?" I ate the last piece of dried meat, taking care not to breathe through my nose.

His muddy green gaze flicked to mine. "Who's Hemeda?"

"The one-handed priestess you abducted. I heard her scream last night. I want to see her."

His brow pinched together as he straightened. "The only one screaming last night was you. You were delirious, calling out for this Hemeda. Who is she to you?"

"Are you saying you didn't send me the box with a copy of the prophecy and a note threatening to expose me if I didn't meet you in the catacombs?"

"I've never sent you a box or a note."

"And you expect me to believe you?"

"Your belief is irrelevant to the truth."

"How did you know I was the wraith if you didn't track down and torture the only living soul who knew my true identity?"

"Your scent. It's unmistakable. I was convinced it was Zwara who'd stabbed me in the alley until I stepped into her chambers and discovered you there." He reached across the table and let his fingertips ghost over a lock of my hair. "Looking at you now, I don't know how I could ever mistake her for you."

The zealot studied me in a way that made my skin heat. For the first time in my life, I missed my cursed veil. Every male in Eden had seen me naked during the rites. None had ever seen my face. I pushed my hair over my shoulder, out of his reach.

"If you knew, why did you insist on interrogating the priestesses?"

His chair groaned as he leaned back. "To find out who else is involved. Dealing frenzy is a dangerous business. I needed to make sure you weren't putting the *ki'sikilta* at risk."

Guilt pricked at my insides like a sea nettle. It was my fault Tesk had caught the wasting. I'd been careful to scrub myself clean after my visits to the lower city, but I'd still managed to bring the toxins back with me. "How is she?"

"Recovered, thanks to you. The Order is in your debt for saving your sister."

I rolled my eyes. "So that's why you haven't taken me to the Rift to be tried for consuming a soul?"

"One of the reasons." He smoothed his beard with his hand. "Why do you sell your frenzy? You don't need the coin. Queens live a life of luxury in the Keep and want for nothing. How did you become a wall-climbing, knife-wielding drug dealer?"

"It's a long story."

"I've got nothing but time. Humor me."

"Like you said, Commander zurNaga, information isn't free, and I'm going to need payment up front. Help me rescue Hemeda, and I'll tell you anything you want to know."

"A hunt and a prize?" The corner of his mouth curled in a cocky smile as he thrust a calloused hand toward me. "You have a deal, wraith. When was the last time you saw her?"

"At her house in the lower city. I went there after I left you in the alley."

"I have someone watching that shack. No one's been in or out in days."

"She must have fled to the goddesses' shrine near the entrance of the catacombs."

"Are you sure? The passages leading to the shrine have been sealed for centuries."

"I found a way in. If we start there, you can pick up her scent and track where they've taken her." My legs felt surprisingly sturdy as I shoved away from the table and headed for the door.

"Not so fast." He stood and untied a strip of black fabric from the grip of his spear. "I need to cover your eyes."

"You're blindfolding me?"

"I can't have you telling Zwara all the Order's secrets when I send you back. You go blindfolded or we don't go at all. I'm sure you understand the precaution."

"You don't trust me?" I asked innocently.

"Not even a little. Turn around."

I gave him my back and let him place the fabric over my face. My pulse raced as his fingers brushed my cheeks. I told myself the fluttering in my chest was a completely normal reaction to being held hostage by my enemy.

He bent close to my ear. "I can smell your distress. Rest assured, you're safe with me, my queen."

"I'd feel safer with a blade." The illustration of a gorzin's open mouth from the book the zealot had given me flashed through my head. The giant sea snakes nested in the caves beneath the catacombs and prowled the tunnels looking for an easy meal. The carcass-crunching scavengers were immune to the wasting and had a taste for Kateri flesh. All teeth, scales, and sinuous muscle, they were adept hunters despite their lack of eyes. More than one body collector had gone missing in my time as the wraith.

"I don't think so. You tried to kill me once already. I'm not giving you a knife so you can put it in my back, wraith." He gripped my elbow and led me through the door. "We need to move quickly and quietly. Stay close and try to keep up."

All I could see through the thick fabric covering my eyes was the blue-green glow from the zealot's chest. He led me silently through the disorienting network of tunnels, hands moving from my elbow to my hip or the small of my back to guide me around obstacles and tripping hazards. I tried to count my steps and memorize each turn, but the corridors tangled like seaweed, and it was impossible to keep track when every nerve in my body was focused on where he touched me.

The loose dirt beneath my feet gave way to cobbled stone and the rush of water as we approached the underground ruins of ancient Eden.

He stopped abruptly, and the soft hairs on my neck rose as he removed my blindfold and pressed a finger to his lips. I stilled at the hiss of scales over stone.

Every instinct screamed at me to run as I glanced over my shoulder. A forked blue tongue as long as my arm tasted the air as an adult gorzin swayed its eyeless head from side to side, listening. I didn't dare breathe, even though I knew the beast could hear my heart slamming against my ribs. The same way I knew we were within striking distance as it opened its milky white mouth and reared back to strike.

"Run."

My chest lit as I bolted down the tunnel behind him, ignoring the searing pain in my lungs. The stone beneath my feet shook as the beast's fanged jaw struck the spot where we'd been standing a moment before. Although the gorzin had a lightning-fast strike, they were slow to recover and give chase. A hunter with healthy lungs could easily outrun them with a head start. I was strong, but my scarred lungs left me at a disadvantage and slowed us both down.

My thundering pulse clogged my ears as we rounded another corner and the narrow corridor opened abruptly to a wide landing overlooking the heart of the abandoned city once ruled by the Nūkiri. I slid to a stop on the damp stone and nearly went careening over the edge.

Brex grabbed my arm and dragged me up a set of steps that spiraled around the cavern walls like a corkscrew connecting one level of the city to the next. "This way. There's a passage behind the falls."

Sweat slicked my face as I did my best to keep up with his long strides. The next landing was on the other side of the raging current that disappeared into the darkness below. I glanced back as the serpent slithered onto the landing and cocked its head toward us.

"It's following us."

The zealot pushed me ahead, and I took the steps two at a time, still moving too slowly. A soft buzzing sensation spread over my skin as he wrapped his shield around me, compelling my feet to move faster.

"Are you trying to kill me?" I said, wheezing and gasping for air.

"We're almost there. The water will break your scent trail. You'll be safe once you're on the other side. I'll be right behind you."

The steps flattened into a ramp pounded smooth over the centuries by the falls. My feet slipped on the algae-slick stone. I hugged the wall, claws grasping for purchase against the smooth rock as the ledge beneath my feet narrowed. Overspray bit my skin like shards of glass as I inched behind the raging torrent.

A growl echoed across the cavern as the gorzin slithered up the steps. I sucked in a breath and stepped behind the wall of water. I pressed my back against the wall and shuffled along the slippery ledge. My fingers ached with the effort it took to cling to the rock.

The lip beneath my feet ended at the edge of the falls where a crevice split the cavern wall and a section of stone had fallen away. I dropped my head back against the rock and exhaled slowly. There was only one way forward. I had to jump.

I lunged across the gap. Pain exploded where my knees smacked against the ground. I scrambled out of the way to make room for the zealot. But Brex wasn't behind me. He was still on the opposite side of the falls, his spear pointed at the approaching beast.

I'd wished him dead more times than I could count, but not like this. At least, that's what I told myself as I picked up a chunk of rock the size of my fist and hurled it at the steps behind the snake. Its head whipped toward the noise. I threw two more rocks farther down as Brex slipped behind the falls. The gorzin slithered down the steps to investigate as the zealot landed on his feet with a thud next to me.

"You have excellent aim. Thanks for the diversion."

"We have a deal, Commander. I couldn't let you get eaten before you held up your end of our agreement."

"Worse creatures have tried to kill me."

"What could possibly be worse than a gorzin?"

"That's a story for another time, my queen."

My hand drifted self-consciously to my middle. "Don't call me that. I'm not a queen anymore."

He was in front of me in two strides. "You will always be a queen." He brought his fist to his chest. "My body and blade are in your debt for the sacrifice you made to save the *ki'sikilta*."

I shoved away from him. "I am in no mood for your holy babble, zealot. If you *ever* restrain me like that again, I will gut you."

"As you say, my queen." His jaw ticked with irritation as he dipped his chin.

The wet tunic clung to my body as I trudged up the steps toward the next landing in silence. Another growl echoed across the cavern. Brex's head snapped to the tunnel we'd exited. The gorzin that attacked us reared and flared its hood. I followed the angle of its cocked head to the landing ahead of us.

Brex pulled me behind him as another serpent slithered out of the archway and coiled itself into a pile. Its head swayed from side to side, searching. It was half the size of the first, but it could still snap a spine with its powerful jaws.

I studied the cavern wall. "Can you climb?"

"Not without a rope."

My wet hair fell forward as I leaned over the edge, calculating the distance to the level below. Too far. Even if we lowered ourselves down, we'd break our legs in the fall.

The snake's head swiveled toward us, catching our scent. We were well within striking distance. Our only chance was to lure it back to the falls and hope the torrent was strong enough to send it plummeting to Wu'uru's tomb at the bottom of the chasm.

"I have a plan." Pebbles skittered down the slope toward us as the snake moved. I didn't have time to explain. The zealot growled a curse as I took off in a dead run.

I braced for the rip of fangs as my body slammed against the wall.

"Don't move," Brex snarled. He had me pinned between the rough rock and his hard chest, my hands trapped at my sides.

The hair on the back of my neck rose as the gorzin hissed fewer than twenty paces away. Well within striking distance.

I bucked against him. "What are you doing? We need to run."

A buzzing sensation kissed my skin, and I went preternaturally still as he dropped his head next to mine. "If you want to live, little wraith, you need to listen to me very carefully. I'm blocking our heartbeats and scents, but the gorzin can detect disturbances in the air caused by sudden movement and loud noise. So we're going to rest here nice and quiet and convince it that we're part of this wall. Blink if you understand."

I flashed him my fangs.

"I'll take that as a yes." His lips twitched as he pressed into me, every part of his body heavy against mine. He cut his eyes to the snake as it scented the air. "I want you to slide your hand up my thigh and slowly unlatch my blade."

Light pulsed from his bare chest as I scraped my claws over his leathers and did as he commanded, having little choice to do otherwise. If I didn't know better, I'd say the zealot was enjoying it. He'd relinquished enough control to allow me to unsheathe his knife. I bit back a smile as I twisted my wrist and pressed the tip to his groin. A silent warning that I wouldn't hesitate to make his vow of celibacy permanent.

His lips grazed my ear. "Careful, wraith. Nothing turns me on more than the threat of violence. I'm going to release control of your body when the beast gets close. If you get a shot at its throat, take it."

I'd never seen a gorzin before today, but I'd read enough to know the spot—the soft flesh in the hollow under its jaw. "Don't hesitate when you strike. Follow through and jam the knife up through the pallet and into its brain."

He didn't flinch as the gorzin's forked tongue flicked over his back. My heart skittered as its featherlight kiss slid along my exposed shoulder. Testing. Tasting.

The gorzin jabbed us with its blunt nose, and for all the zealot's chiseled muscle, he was not made of stone. His body rocked, and the beast reared back, spreading its hood.

"Now." He released me from his shield and grabbed the spear strapped to his back. The gorzin's frothy white maw stretched wide, revealing fangs as long as my hands. A scream tore from my throat as its head came down. I thrust the blade into its mouth and felt it pierce bone. My entire body reverberated with the impact, knocking me to my knees as something warm and wet poured down my arm.

I had enough sense to let go of the knife and yank my arm back before its jaw snapped shut. Brex cinched an arm around my waist and pulled me out of the way as the snake's body spasmed violently. The silver tip of the knife protruded from its skull.

"You're all right. I've got you."

He held me until the animal's twitching body went still. I only realized I was trembling when he released me.

The zealot's brow furrowed as he stroked the beast's nose and recited something in the old language before reaching inside its mouth. It was impossible to ignore the way his back flexed as he worked to pull the blade free.

"You speak ancient Kateri?"

"Everyone in the Order can recite a few blessings."

"Did you just bless the monster that tried to kill us?"

"You can't fault a creature for doing what's in its nature. We're all just trying to survive."

I wasn't sure what it was about his words that unsettled me more. The calmness with which he said them, or the way they settled like a weight in my chest.

We continued in silence to the salt catacombs. I led him to the south exit beneath the lower city. The sun painted the sea and sky red as it dipped beneath the horizon. The body collectors would arrive soon with their overladen carts.

Brex followed me around the cliff's edge to the hidden alcove overlooking the ocean.

"The shrine is down there." I pointed to a fissure in the bedrock.

"How did you find this?"

"I snuck out here after I killed my first mate. Hemeda followed me and talked me off the ledge. We found the shrine by accident. It's an easy climb. The crystals jut out from the wall like pegs, but they like to break off. Make sure your weight is distributed on more than one anchor point as you descend." I moved to lower myself into the shaft.

"Wait." He thrust his arm in front of me as he smelled the air. His scowl told me something was off.

"What's wrong?" All I could hear was the gentle slosh of waves against the cliff far below.

"Nothing. I should go in alone. Your scent will overpower whatever lingers down there."

"Is that your way of telling me I stink?" I asked, letting my shoulders relax.

"On the contrary, my queen." Brex squeezed his big body into the crevice. "Stay here."

I paced under the overhang, listening for signs of trouble. The commander came up almost as quickly as he'd gone down.

"Did you pick up her scent?"

"No. Let's go." He ushered me away from the open shaft.

"What do you mean, no? You were only down there for a moment." I pointed his blade toward the hole. "You said you were the best tracker in Eden. Go back and sniff around until you find something."

"There's no need." He let out a heavy sigh. "There's no easy way to say this. Your friend is dead."

"Get out of my way." I tried to push past him. Hemeda couldn't be dead. The zealot had to be mistaken.

"I'm afraid I can't do that." He wrapped his arms around me.

"Let me go." Angry tears spilled down my cheeks as I flashed my fangs and pummeled his chest with my fists.

"Look at me." He cupped my face in his palms. "There are things that can never be unseen. I won't allow what's down there to be the last memory you have of your friend."

"I'm going to destroy whoever did this." A blood rage pulsed across my bioluminescent markings.

His brow pinched as he stroked my hair. "There are several broken pegs inside the shaft, and her injuries are consistent with a fall. For what it's worth, I don't think she suffered for long."

I didn't need any help conjuring the image of Hemeda's twisted body lying at the goddesses' feet. A sob tore from my throat as my knees buckled. She was gone, and it was my fault. Hemeda was good. She didn't deserve to die.

"It should have been me," I hissed.

Brex sank to the ground with me as I retreated into myself.

"Breathe, Vaza." His mouth was at my ear, but his voice was far away. I fell through the dark into the empty clutch at my core. The place I forced my mind to go, where pain and duty didn't exist. Where the souls I once carried would press in and protect me from feeling anything at all during the rite. Except there were no souls left to break my fall. Just a hollowed-out shell.

A gentle vibration hummed against my chest, coaxing me back toward the light. Brex held me in his lap, with my head tucked into his shoulder. I let out a shuddering breath, and his arms tightened around me. No one had ever held me like that. Gentle and firm all at once.

My body—my entire being—ached with fatigue. I was so tired of duty and death and not being able to escape any of it. It would be easy to curl into him and pretend, for a moment, that none of it mattered. That this male, with his unsettling tenderness, wasn't my enemy. That he didn't want to sacrifice my sister to his dead god.

I swiped at my tears and peeled myself away from him.

"'Don't let your death be insignificant.' That was the last thing she said to me." I stared out at the stars pricking to life against the darkening sky.

"Do you want to talk about it?"

I shook my head, not trusting my voice to answer without betraying me.

"I wish I could say it gets better. It doesn't. Greif fades. The guilt will always be with you." His face pinched in pain. "You'll never stop feeling responsible for the ones you couldn't save."

We sat in silence for a long time, watching the sky fade from blue to black and listening to the tide break against the impenetrable wall below. My ass had gone numb. I shifted so the glowing crevice was no longer in my periphery.

The zealot eyed me as he stretched out his legs and leaned against the wall. "The caves will be crawling with body collectors by now. We should wait here until morning. Try to get some rest. I'll keep watch."

"I don't think I can turn my mind off long enough to fall asleep."

"Will you allow me to distract you with a story about the Nūkiri and the god of tides?"

I cut him a sideways glance. "So you do intend to torture me."

"They were lovers before they became enemies."

I gave an incredulous grunt. "Not according to the history books."

"Books written by the Order. They made sure the narrative portrayed the god of tides as an infallible deity worthy of devotion. In truth, he was anything but. When he came to Eden, he was young and impulsive. He possessed all seven mage abilities and made a show of wielding them. He spent his days protecting hunting pods and whaling parties from the red tide and his nights in the public baths, drinking and fucking. No one went hungry and the city became enamored with their bawdy new god.

"The Nūkiri invited him to their palace and threw lavish parties in his honor. He became entranced by their beauty and distracted by the pleasures of court life. The goddesses made him their personal consort and gave him a seat on their dais. The god of tides ruled at their side until Wu'uru, the Nūkiri's favorite seer, had a vision that changed the course of his fate.

"He predicted the red tide would destroy Eden and that the god of tides would find his Gi'dari—his one true mate—among those infected with the wasting. That their bond would snap into place a moment before she died. The Nūkiri dismissed the prophet's vision, as they often did when it didn't pertain to or benefit them in any way. The city was thriving under their rule, and they had the god of tides under their seductive spell. There was no reason to believe it would ever change.

"The god of tides, however, took it to heart and started spending more and more time away from the palace. He devoted his gifts to working in the temple with the blood mages, doing what he could to treat and give comfort to those infected with the wasting."

"Did he find his Gi'dari?" I asked, annoyed that I was actually invested in this obvious fabrication. The irrevocable bond between two souls was a thing of fables and myth. It didn't happen in real life.

The zealot shook his head. "The goddesses demanded he give them his full attention. When he refused them, they sucked out nearly all of his power and made him watch as they fed every wasting survivor and female that he'd ever shown an interest in to their pet gorzin."

"Okay, stop. That's clearly an embellishment. How does someone keep a gorzin as a pet?"

"With a constant supply of fresh meat and a very large pool." Brex lobbed a pebble over the edge of the cliff. "Every female at court started wearing veils to avoid being cursed by his gaze. The goddesses punished anyone he accidentally looked at for too long. Fear of the Nūkiri was so strong the tradition of wearing veils persisted. It's why the queens still wear them to this day.

"The Nūkiri dosed him with frenzy and forced him to service their needs. When they tired of using his body for their own pleasure, they threw him into the pool with their pets. He killed three of them before suffering a mortal wound. The goddesses had him strung up outside the palace where everyone could watch him bleed to death.

"Wu'uru and his followers cut down the god of tides' body and made him their martyr. The rest you know. The Nūkiri imprisoned the prophet in their dungeon, where he wrote the prophecy and planned the coup that ended their cruel reign."

I rolled my eyes. "The Order would convert more followers if you fed them this debaucherous version of your dead god." I yawned as I lay on my back, still gripping his blade in one hand. "He's far more interesting than the pious prick who demands celibacy and sacrifice from his disciples."

"Everyone who joins the Order learns the truth. The sacrifices they make during the ordeal create bonds between members. The vow helps them remain focused. We wouldn't have endured this long without that level of loyalty and discipline." He chucked another rock off the cliff. "When the prophecy is fulfilled and the god of tides is restored, the faithful will be rewarded."

"Is that what they tell you to justify the long, lonely nights with nothing to keep you company but your own calloused hand?"

His chest flashed with anger. "I just told you all my secrets, wraith. Don't tempt me to cut out your vicious tongue."

I bit back a smile as I rolled on my side and faced the wall, thankful the zealot's moods shifted faster than a targul's skin. Grumpy and self-righteous I could handle. It felt safe and not the least bit unsettling.

Chapter Eight
VAZA

"Well, isn't this cozy?" A deep male voice pulled me out of a dreamless sleep, and I was immediately aware of three things.

The zealot's leather-clad thigh beneath my cheek, the golden light creeping over the horizon, and the pale prince leering down at me. A blond female in matching black armor appeared behind him. I recognized her as the mind mage who'd faked an injury in Zwara's office. Half of her golden hair had been pulled back in a sloppy knot. The rest cascaded in waves down her back. They both carried spears and were strapped with knives.

"How'd you find us?" Brex asked as I sat up and scooted away from him.

"We followed the trail of blood. Thought you might have run into trouble."

"We were attacked by a gorzin," he said, voice raspy with sleep. "Fortunately, the queen knows how to handle a blade."

"You were supposed to keep her in her cell until we came for her. Not give her a weapon and take her hunting."

"I needed some fresh air." The zealot stood and offered me his hand. Our eyes locked in silent acknowledgment of the lie. "You know I don't like being underground."

He didn't tell them about Hemeda or me being the wraith. He'd kept my secret safe.

"Friends of yours?" I grasped his palm and let him pull me to my feet.

"This is Hazi, my second in the Order Guard, and Inanna, a silent disciple of the god of tides."

Inanna gave me a tight-lipped smile as she dipped her head, and I realized why I'd never heard her speak. She'd chosen the pilgrimage to Wu'uru's tomb as her ordeal and lost her tongue for the privilege.

"Has the high priestess agreed to our terms?" Brex asked as he brushed the dirt off his pants.

"She made a counteroffer," Hazi said.

Brex glanced at the mind mage and scowled at whatever she'd projected into his head. "Tell her we have a deal."

"It's too much," Hazi said.

Brex shot him a daggered glance. "It's not up for discussion."

"Can someone please tell me what's going on?"

"Your presence is required at the temple." The prince's voice went tight. "The high priestess has reinstated the rite."

"You must be mistaken. Zwara would never reinstate the mating rite during a red tide. She won't have any meat to feed the hatchlings."

I couldn't see the prince's markings beneath his leather armor, but there was no mistaking the disgust that contorted his elegant features. "She's not planning on feeding the hatchlings. She's brought back the sacrificial rite."

My body went hot and woozy as the contents of my stomach crawled up my throat. The cannibalistic practice hadn't been used to survive the red tide since the time of the Nūkiri. The goddesses frequently spawned broods of soulless hatchlings to feed the population.

I bent forward and braced my hands on my knees, willing the nausea to quell. "Does Tesk know?"

"The only thing they've been told is that the mating rite has been reinstated and their mates have been selected."

Niva would already be preparing Tesk for the ritual, anointing her body with oil, threading pearls into her long hair, and sweeping it up into a braided crown to keep her neck and shoulders free for her mate's fangs. She was likely delirious with excitement. She had no idea what would be asked of her.

My hand went to my abdomen as I straightened. "Why would Zwara summon *me* to the rite if I'm no longer able to spawn?"

"You're to be made an example of," Brex said. "A reminder to the other queens of the consequences of non-compliance. After I took you, the high priestess made a public announcement that the Order took you to be cruciated as punishment for stealing a soul."

"And the Order went along with it?" I asked.

"We didn't really have a choice," Hazi said, clasping the commander on the shoulder. "Do you want to ask her, or shall I?"

"Ask me what?"

"We need your help," Brex said.

I crossed my arms over my chest. "This should be interesting. Do tell me how I can assist you after you abducted me and held me for ransom."

"I need you to convince the *ki'sikilta* not to participate in the mating ceremony."

"You want me to help you preserve her for the prophecy?" I laughed as I glanced back and forth between the three of them. "No. Now get out of my fucking way."

Hazi and Inanna crossed their spears, blocking my path.

"Let me pass."

"I'm afraid we can't do that," the prince said.

"You're all fools if you think Zwara would give Tesk the option of declining. She would have cruciated me herself if the guard's knife hadn't done the job for her. Do not underestimate her wrath. She would never allow a queen to undermine her authority by rejecting the rite."

"That's why you're going to take her place," Brex said behind me.

I spun on my heels to face him.

"Why would I do that? The sooner Tesk is mated, the better. I'll not help you sacrifice my sister to your dead fucking god."

"The *ki'sikilta* must make the sacrifice willingly. The prophecy is clear on that point. We can't force it upon her. When the time comes, it will be her choice. You have my word."

"Why should I believe you?"

"Because our *dead* god would never condone forcing a female to do anything against her will." Light pulsed from his chest, and goddess help me, I wanted to believe him.

"There's only one problem." I gestured to the collection of silver scars that covered my body. "Tesk and I aren't completely identical."

"Inanna can take care of that," Hazi said.

I felt another brush against the back of my mind and glanced down at my bare arms. The bite marks on my chest and shoulders—one for every male who'd claimed me against my will—disappeared.

"Stay out of my head, mage." I flashed her my fangs, and the illusion evaporated. "Even if you can fool Zwara and an entire temple full of spectators, Tesk's mate won't be so easily deceived. He'll have paid an exorbitant fee for the pleasure of being the first to claim her. My gills were destroyed by the wasting. As soon as he pulls me under the water, he'll know something's wrong."

"We've taken care of that as well." The prince gave me a dry look. "You'll hear no complaints from the mate Zwara contracted for your sister."

The Order disdained the way Zwara used the mating rite to exert political control over the city. She'd be suspicious if they were in any way connected to the male. Which meant they'd likely paid the cost for a lesser noble or even a merchant who couldn't afford to bid against the four houses in return for his silence.

"Who did you bribe?" I demanded.

"Does it matter?" the zealot asked through clenched teeth. "You'll be saving your sister from spawning a brood of soulless hatchings for slaughter. All you need to do is get through the rite without ripping out your mate's throat."

My neck cracked as I tilted my head from side to side, considering my options. Let Zwara use me to keep the other queens in line and watch as some lecherous male claimed my sister and removed the burden of being the last virgin queen from her shoulders. Or save Tesk from the horrors of having to sacrifice her first brood of hatchlings and allow the Order to maintain their hope in the prophecy. If the story Brex told me was true, Wu'uru had been wrong before. He'd falsely predicted the red tide would bring about the fall of Eden and that the god of tides would find his mythical Gi'dari. Neither had come to pass.

"I have conditions."

The zealot squared his shoulders. "Name your price."

"We tell Tesk everything. She makes the final decision, and no one says a word to her about prophecies or destiny or resurrecting the god of tides. I'll not let you brainwash her into becoming one of your disciples. If she agrees to the switch and this plan of yours goes sideways, I want your word that you'll protect her from Zwara's wrath."

"We have a deal, my queen." His rough calluses scraped against mine as he grasped my outstretched palm.

⁓

The commander's shoulder jabbed into my middle as he climbed the tight circular staircase to the high priestess's private chambers with me slung over his back. Hazi suggested it'd be more believable if it looked like I'd resisted. Brex disagreed. As a shield, he could compel my body to follow his commands. He insisted the rough treatment wasn't necessary and had immediately been outvoted by everyone. Including me. Zwara lived to see me suffer. It was sure to put her in a pleasant mood.

His claws dug into the backs of my thighs. "Careful, zealot. If your fingers slide any higher, you'll be in danger of breaking your sacred vows." I let my eyes crawl over the leathers that hugged the curve of his ass and powerful thighs.

"Stop wiggling. Your sweaty legs are hard to hold on to."

"It's cute that you think that's sweat." I couldn't hide the way my body reacted to his touch, especially when he could smell the slightest changes in my moods.

"I was being polite. You could at least pretend my life isn't a joke to you."

We rounded the top of the staircase before I could respond. A pair of priestesses smirked as they opened the doors to Zwara's chambers.

The zealot dumped me unceremoniously on the floor. "The Order agrees to your terms, your highness."

I hissed at the male as I shoved up to my feet. Brex stretched his neck, as if lugging me up to my sister's chambers had been a heavy burden. I couldn't tell whether it was genuine or for my wicked sister's benefit. He had so many dissonant personalities he was impossible to read. He flipped between grumpy zealot, tender protector, and seductive courtier so often I had no idea which one was real.

Zwara straightened from where she hunched over a pile of old scrolls with her personal consort. All three of Kor's forms bristled at the interruption.

"I see she's overstayed her welcome. Thank you for returning her in one piece, Commander. I'm sure the Order has much to prepare. You may leave us."

"I live to serve, your highness." He gave her a stiff bow and didn't spare so much as a glance in my direction. A strange tugging sensation pulled at my chest as I watched him leave.

"You're wondering why you're here," Zwara said as she leaned against the table next to Kor's beautiful female form, all long, lustrous legs and slender features.

"I'm assuming you've invented new ways to torture me," I said dryly.

"I've gone to great lengths to ensure you, Tesk, and the other queens have every luxury while the rest of Eden slowly starves to death. So, dear sister, I'll ask you to check your tone when you speak to me."

"Your guard *cruciated* me."

Her icy blue eyes narrowed. "You sealed your own fate when you consumed a soul entrusted to your care."

"Don't pretend you're not thrilled that I saved your little jewel and that you haven't sold her off to the highest bidder for the sacrificial rite."

"Your recklessness is not without its merits." Zwara twisted and picked up a small, freshly sealed scroll from the table. A contract for a queen's matings. "My sources tell me the Order is transporting supplies from the Rift to the underground city. Is it true?"

"What makes you think I'd know anything about the zealots and their agenda?" I asked as I sauntered over to the tank of live scuttle crabs between the jeweled-glass eyes that overlooked the temple's mating pools. I tapped on the tank and watched the fat, clawed crustaceans scurry away.

"Don't play coy with me, Vaza. I know you're planning to switch places with your sister in the rite." I plastered an expressionless mask over my face as she continued. "Prince Hazi came to me with the idea when I opened bids for the queens. I thought it was absurd at first, but they made me an offer I couldn't refuse."

"I'm curious. Exactly how much is maintaining her virginity worth?"

"Their payment was far more valuable than just coin." She tapped a claw against the scroll in her hand. "I allowed them to buy out Tesk's participation in exchange for you *and* their unprecedented support of the rite."

"So it's a win-win for everyone except the queens."

"Why does it not surprise me that's all you would see? Hate me if you must, but everything I've ever done has been to keep this city from collapsing."

The stench of dried gorzin blood climbed up my nose as I scrubbed my hands over my face. "And you assumed I would just go along with the plan."

"Of course not." Zwara rounded the table and took her seat. "In exchange for your cooperation, you'll be absolved of your crime and allowed to resume your title and privileges as a queen. You'll be permitted to move back into the Keep, and you'll have the freedom to come and go as you like and consort with whomever you please."

"How did you convince Tesk to go along with this scheme?"

"I'll leave that to you. Your reunion with her is my gift to you for helping her make the right decision should she get any disobedient notions. One of the temple guards will escort you back to the House of Blood to prepare. I expect you to put on a good show for the crowd. You might try letting yourself enjoy it for once."

I bit back the response that would do me no favors and dipped my head instead. I'd never allowed a male to claim my pleasure, and I certainly wasn't going to start now. It was the only thing they couldn't take without my consent.

"Do give your lovely sister our regards." Kor's female form blew me a kiss as I left.

 VAZA

Niva hummed a comforting tune as she wove Tesk's iridescent hair into an intricate crown. My sister's slumped shoulders told me she already knew the horror of what the queens were being forced to do.

Zwara and the Order could go fuck themselves. I didn't trust the high priestess any more than I trusted the zealots. I didn't owe any of them my loyalty. The only one who mattered in any of this was Tesk. No matter which way this went, she would be the one to suffer. Participate in the sacrificial rite and spend the rest of her life regretting it or agree to the switch and hope the zealots kept their word about offering her a choice. Whatever happened, it would be Tesk's decision. She was the one at the center of this tangled knot, and she had a right to choose her own fate.

The crisscrossing cords holding the narrow front and back panels of my waist-drape in place dug into my hips as I approached my sister. She wore a matching ceremonial set. Triangles of black silk covered her full breasts. My too-tight skin itched from being scrubbed raw by the priestesses. They'd even scraped out the dried gorzin blood from beneath my claws, which I couldn't stop extending and retracting.

I waved Niva away and took over the task of pinning my sister's braids.

"Your tits are definitely bigger than mine," I said, attempting to keep my voice from wavering.

Tesk whipped around and immediately turned into a blubbering mess, smearing the kohl that lined her eyes and streaking the mica powder that had been dusted over her cheeks. She leapt from the stool and hugged me, knocking me back two paces. I curled around her, biting back hot tears of my own.

I wasn't sure how long we clung to each other, but she was the first to pull away. Her eyes dropped to my bare midriff and low-slung skirt. She ghosted her fingers over the thick rope of scar tissue. "At least Zwara didn't silver it."

"I don't think she had time. How are your gills?" I asked, lifting her arm out of the way to inspect them.

"I'd rather you let me die," she whispered.

My chest pinched. "Please, don't say that."

"What they're making us do. It's not right."

"I know." I used my thumb to clean her cheeks. "Take a walk with me in the garden?"

Tesk nodded silently and hooked her arm through mine. Our guards followed twenty paces behind as we made our way out of the Keep to the House of Blood's medicinal gardens.

Crushed shells bleached from the sun crunched beneath our feet as we wound around beds of desiccated plants. There weren't enough blood mages left to tend the flowers and herbs. The once beautiful garden had become a grave of broken stems. No one came out here anymore. Especially at night, when it took on an eerie chill. There were no witnesses to see me scale the garden wall and disappear into the lower city.

"You don't have to participate in the rite," I said.

"Are you finally offering to sneak me out of the Keep?" She tucked her head against my shoulder with a huff.

I kept my voice low as I relayed my conversation with Zwara and the deal I'd made with the Order. "They have a mind mage who'll take care of the minor differences in our appearances. If you agree, you won't be forced to spawn your first pod of hatchlings for slaughter."

She stopped abruptly. "You would do that for me?"

I grasped her hands. "Only if it's what you desire. If you don't agree to the switch, I can help you escape the Keep right now. If you go to the Rift, the Order will offer you refuge."

"Since when do you trust the zealots?"

"I trust the commander to protect you from Zwara's wrath. You'll have to remain their *ki'sikilta* for a little longer, but—"

"Vaza, I'm not worried about the prophecy anymore. I'm not their *ki'sikilta*." Tesk stared at our clasped hands. "I'm not a virgin."

"Getting yourself off with a crystal phallus doesn't count. You need to be claimed by a mate."

Tesk's lips quirked with amusement. "Then I am triple not a virgin."

I glanced around and pulled her under the twisted branches of a dead tree.

"What are you saying?"

She glanced over her shoulder before pulling her waist-drape to the side, revealing three silver bite marks high on her inner thigh. "I'm saying I made a deal of my own."

"Zwara's going to make your life miserable for this."

"Who do you think arranged it? She gave us her chambers for the night and made a tonic to prevent me from spawning. Kor was..." Tesk's cheeks flushed as a bright smile lit her face. "They were gentle and... extremely attentive."

"Kor? As in all three of them? At once?"

"Don't be so judgy."

"I'm not being judgy."

"Your face says otherwise. I can see you scowling through your veil."

"I'm thrilled for you. But we'll lose the Order's protection the moment they learn you're not their precious virgin."

Tesk hushed me and pulled me back to the path as our escort neared.

"Then we won't tell them until it's absolutely necessary. Let them play their political games with Zwara. I'm just glad you're alive. The commander snapped and went into a blood frenzy after you saved me. He disemboweled a guard with one swipe of his claws."

"He killed a guard?" I rubbed at the tightness in my chest that refused to ease.

"The one who threw the knife. I've never seen anyone as enraged as he was when he took you away. Zwara said the Order wanted to punish you for consuming a soul."

"It was a lie to cover up the embarrassment of allowing a queen to be abducted from right under her nose."

"So he didn't torture you?"

"I suppose that depends on your definition. He forced me to eat salted meat and listen to stories about the god of tides." I didn't tell her about Hemeda. That was a conversation I still wasn't ready to have.

"You mean to tell me that I've been worrying myself sick for five days imagining all the horrific ways the Order could be punishing you, and all this time, the commander was nursing you back to health?" Tesk punched my shoulder.

"There was no nursing. He sat in a corner and kept watch to make sure I didn't die and ruin the Order's negotiations with the high priestess. He needed me alive so I could take your place in the rite. The only thing he cares about is preserving the prophecy."

"Zwara won't leave anything to chance," Tesk said. "She'll have chosen a mate who can control you if you go into a blood frenzy. I can't ask you to go through that again."

The bell tolled from the temple, announcing the call to the rites. I pulled Tesk into what would appear to anyone watching as a hug of condolence. "I'll be fine. Let me do this for you."

❧

"I can't tell them apart," Hazi said as he circled us in Zwara's chambers, studying the mind mage's work.

Inanna's brow pinched in concentration as she looked back and forth between Tesk and me, inspecting our matching silver scars. I held out my arms and watched as mine vanished one by one. My chest pinched as I ran my hands over my pristine skin, wishing I could erase the memories just as easily. Would they fade with time without the constant reminder of what had been taken from me over and over again?

"Are you all right?" Tesk placed a steady hand on my shoulder.

"I'm…" I cleared my throat. "The illusion is perfect," I said, turning to the prince. "Someone needs to play prison guard and escort Tesk to the high priestess's dais," I said. "Commander zurNaga promised he'd keep her safe."

"It will be my honor to escort the *ki'sikilta*."

"No offense, princeling, but I'd be more comfortable if it was Brex. If anything goes wrong, Tesk's safety is the priority."

"Brex may be able to compel your heart to keep beating and bring you back from the brink of death, but I can compel an entire temple of spectators to stop breathing under my shield."

"What did you just say?"

"The *ki'sikilta* is safer with me."

"No. The other thing about Brex… keeping my heart beating."

His eyes darted to Inanna and back to me. "It was just an example. Inanna will escort you to the mating pool, where she'll bear witness along with your handmaiden to ensure the mating contract is fulfilled. Zwara ordered her to project the claiming to the crowd," Hazi said in a clipped tone. "Her highness couldn't resist the opportunity to publicly discredit the Order by ensuring everyone witnesses the defilement of the *ki'sikilta*."

The mind mage flashed her teeth and spat on the ground in agreement.

"Are you sure you can maintain three projections at once?" Tesk asked Inanna.

The humorless smirk she shot my sister told me she didn't enjoy being second-guessed any more than Hazi.

"Put your worry to rest, my queen," the prince said to Tesk. "Inanna is the best mind mage in Eden. She'll take care of the crowd. All you need to do is play the part of the nefarious sister." His face turned somber. "Vaza will have the most difficult role. If she tries to murder her mate, the ruse will be over and all of this will have been for nothing."

"That only happened once, and it was an accident," Tesk said, coming to my defense. She wove her fingers through mine as we followed them down the spiral stairs inside the god of tides' hollow body to join the other queens in the temple's narthex. Acolytes pulled a succession of thick ropes connected to the temple's bells. Their too-thin bodies lifted from the ground with each note, announcing the queens' procession.

The clamor of voices fell silent. Tesk and I fell in line behind the others. Me wearing my sister's virgin skin and Tesk covered in my silver scars.

Ice mages stood at the end of each long pool that stretched away from the center aisle. There were too many hollow cheeks and bony ribs in the crowd. Bodies leaned against pillars and each other for support. Whispers grew to a palpable buzz as we passed. All eyes were on Tesk's unveiled face. She held her head high, playing the part of a fallen queen and flashing her fangs at anyone who sneered. The tightness in my chest eased at the fierce glint in her eyes, and I let myself hope we might actually pull off the ruse.

As promised, the entire Order Guard had turned out in full regalia. My stomach did an anxious flip as I scanned the sea of armed warriors. The incessant tugging sensation in my chest eased as my eyes landed on the commander. His hair had been braided back, away from his face, intensifying the set of his clenched jaw.

My gut twisted as he held my gaze. This scheme to keep the virgin queen pure—everything he'd put his faith in—was a lie. If the Order found out the high priestess had double-crossed them, they had enough soldiers present to stage a coup and take the temple.

Zwara sat on a backless throne atop the high dais at the head of the temple. Kor sprawled across the steps below. Each queen bowed to the high priestess before retreating to their individual mating pools. Kor's eyes followed Tesk as Hazi made a show of compelling her to climb the steps and kneel at Zwara's feet.

I swallowed the bile pressing at the back of my throat and bowed to my vicious sister. Inanna followed me to the last round pool where Niva waited.

Zwara stood and addressed the crowd. "It is not with a light heart that I invoke the sacrificial rite. The wasting has taken a great toll on all of us, especially our revered queens, who carry the heaviest burden as the caretakers of our fallen brothers and sisters. As you can see, the Order are here in an unprecedented show of support to assure us that the god of tides has granted his blessing to the queens for the sacrifice they will make today on our behalf. Let us pay our respects to him for this gift."

A collective rumble of movement rolled through the temple as every able body took a knee. Zwara offered a prayer for a productive rite, and it was all I could do to keep from vomiting.

One by one, she called our mates to the dais, where she gave them the traditional blessing of virility. It appeared that size had been prioritized over all other genetic factors in the mate selections, and it made me sick to consider why. I forced my attention to the towering effigy standing watch at the back of the temple. The deity I'd offered my body and soul to in my desperate attempt to save Tesk's life. I glared at the glowing yellow eyes that doubled as windows into Zwara's private chambers.

Hemeda used to say the soul resided behind the eyes. The soul that lived behind the jeweled windows was a cold, manipulative cunt. She was also the only high priestess in history who'd managed to bring the Order to its knees. I'd never admit it to her face, but deep down, I was impressed.

"Brex zurNaga, honored commander and faithful disciple of the Order of Wu'uru, please approach the dais to receive your blessing," Zwara called.

The temple went silent, and I was sure everyone could hear the pulse thudding in my chest as my eyes cut to where he stood in the crowd. I must have heard her wrong. A member of the Order had *never* participated in the rite. Not once.

A rolling wave of hushed voices spread through the stunned spectators as the zealot stepped into the aisle. A quick scan of the other queens' pools told me what I already knew. The Order's presence at the rite wasn't enough for Zwara. She'd gone out of her way to mate their most vocal member to the virgin queen. Zwara wanted everyone to know she was in complete control.

I cut my eyes to Inanna. "This is why the negotiations took so long."

She offered a sympathetic nod.

Fire flared in my gut, and my whole body went hot with rage. "How long has he known we'd be mated?"

I felt a gentle brush at the back of my mind as she projected her voice into my head. "From the beginning."

A jolt ran through my body as Brex's eyes locked with mine.

All you need to do is get through the rite without ripping out your mate's throat.

He'd watched me sacrifice myself to save Tesk and knew I'd do anything to protect her. That I wouldn't say no to the switch. What he couldn't predict was whether the killer queen would try to end him.

"He won't restrain you or make you do anything against your will," Inanna offered. "I'm here to make sure the crowd witnesses what the high priestess wants them to see. As long as you stand close to him, I can fill in the rest."

"That won't be necessary." I curled my lips back, revealing my fangs. There was more than one way to break a zealot. "I thoroughly intend to make him break his vow."

CHAPTER TEN

RENAE

I TIGHTENED AND RETIED the T-shirt around my chest, binding my breasts with the best facsimile of a sports bra I could manage. I'd have to run to make it to the lagoon and back before Liam came back from his studio. My chest ached when I thought about why he was there. We hadn't talked about the drugs in the days since he'd told me.

Addiction was as much mental as it was physical. It didn't matter that these bodies weren't real and that his chemical dependence was a figment of the Void's grip on his psyche. His cravings and withdrawal symptoms felt as real to him as the bruises on my body. I'd promised I wouldn't give up on him. The only way I could keep that promise was by finding a way home where he could get the help and support he needed.

I had no idea how we were going to escape without an Astral. Ziggy had forgotten to mention that little detail in the chaos before she ripped one open and sent me into the Void to save her son.

Not knowing the fates of Liam's mother, who was also my handler, Cyrena the meddling assassin, and my sister Lucy had eaten a hole in my stomach—one made worse by the scenarios I imagined when I let myself think about the Astral we'd hijacked and destroyed. Time ticked slower in Almega. They were likely still fighting their way out or getting captured. Or worse.

I couldn't allow myself to dwell on the punishment the Nūkiri would hand down for disobeying a direct order. If Liam and I made it out of the Void, we'd have to deal with the consequences of my betrayal.

The sky outside the bathroom window darkened with the threat of an approaching storm. Foul weather rolled across the island whenever Liam retreated to his studio, and I suspected it wasn't by chance. The weather responded to his emotions and bent to his will. The twice daily storms were his way of confining me to the bungalow while he was indisposed.

Part of me was impressed by how far his forecasting ability had advanced. The other part of me, the one fed up with his overprotective antics, shoved that sentiment down as I stuffed my silver braid through the back of his baseball cap and tugged it low over my forehead.

His studio was a twenty-minute stroll down the beach from the bungalow. The round trip plus the time he spent there after shooting up gave me a three-hour window to get to the lagoon, explore, and get back in time to wash off the intense fire and brimstone stench. It was stronger there than anywhere else I'd mapped. The only other time I'd gotten anything that strong was during the first few seconds I fed on Liam before his projections covered the taste. They had to be connected. I just needed to get to the bottom of the lagoon to find out how.

Drizzle soaked my skin as I stretched my calves on the porch steps. I felt stronger after feeding on Liam for a few days, but the long hours spent hunched over a pile of reeds and rope had twisted my body into knots.

Static prickled over my skin, raising the hair on my arms as the sound of cracking sticks and rustling leaves erupted behind me. I whipped around, expecting to see Liam stalking out of the rainforest to lecture me about leaving the house without him. There was no one there. A gentle tug on the bond told me he was still in the studio.

I blinked in disbelief as roots rose from the ground, twisting and weaving to form a wall around the house like the ones that made up the wall around the lagoon. He wouldn't...